SWAMP WATER

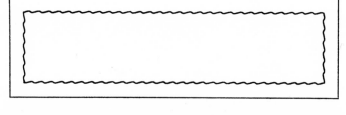

SWAMP WATER

BY VEREEN BELL

Foreword by Vereen Bell, Jr.

The University of Georgia Press

ATHENS

© 1940, 1941 by Vereen Bell
Foreword by Vereen Bell, Jr., copyright © 1981
by the University of Georgia Press
Published by The University of Georgia Press
Athens, Georgia 30602
www.ugapress.org

The Library of Congress has cataloged the hardcover edition
of this book as follows:
Library of Congress Cataloging-in-Publication Data

Bell, Vereen, 1911–1944.
    Swamp water / by Vereen Bell ; foreword by Vereen Bell, Jr.
xvii, 262 p. ; 22 cm.
    ISBN 0-8203-0553-7; 0-8203-0546-4 (pbk.)
    "Brown thrasher books."
    I. Title.

PS3503.E4389 S9   1981   813'.54 19   80-24570
Paperback reissue 2008 ISBN-13: 978-0-8203-3269-7
ISBN-10: 0-8203-3269-0

Swamp Water appeared serially in the *Saturday Evening Post* from
November 23, 1940, to December 18, 1940. Little, Brown and
Company, Boston, published the novel in 1941.

Cover: Scene from the 1941 movie *Swamp Water* starring Dana
Andrews and Walter Brennan. Photography courtesy of the
Museum of Modern Art, Film Still Archives.

FOREWORD

HARD as it is for such a disconcerting truth to sink in, by virtue of my father's having died at the age of thirty-three I am now some twelve years his senior. Moreover, since he died when I was ten, most of what I know about him I have been told by other people. Except for the few firsthand memories of being with him, I find it difficult now to think of him as at all fatherly. I remember riding his back, terrified, as he walked us through a cypress swamp—perhaps in an edge of the Okefenokee—across a sagging and meandering "bridge" made of single eight-inch planks anchored end to end against the cypress trunks. I remember his

v

promising to give me a gold watch like his own if I would not smoke cigarettes until I became a man. (Cynically I began smoking anyway at sixteen; no gold watch, obviously, would be forthcoming.) I remember being admonished frequently for telling lies, which I did frequently—not expedient or conniving ones but those of the tall-tale genre that enhanced ordinary life and my stature in it. (I once asked my mother if she could draw a gorilla in a tree so as to resemble a photograph which I could then show to disbelieving friends, whom I had told I had seen a gorilla in a tree.) This particular character trait of mine I was later told by my kin had a recognizable genetic source. My father was a skillful and serious horseman, and I therefore learned to ride very large horses when I was very small; these were enduring lessons also in not being afraid. In a cherished family photograph, he is gallantly and casually posed upon a sleek chestnut gelding with black mane and tail, named Pat. We hunted and fished together, though never even close to enough for me. He owned a small cabin-cruiser at St. Marks, Florida, called the *Gulf Queen*, and one of my memories is of spending a glorious night on that boat, anchored, rolling in the gulf water under the stars. One of his best friends in that part of the country was a state trooper who caught and rode porpoises and sea turtles for fun—an awesome and vivid man, and not somebody you would be likely even to believe in the existence of if you had had someone else for a father. Later, during the war, I remember being lifted by my father into the cockpit of a Grumman F4F Wildcat, in a very serious violation of Navy regulations. This was in Oregon at a naval air station where he was in training. My mother and younger brother and I had followed him there for what turned out to be our last year together. He could have remained stateside as a gunnery instructor for the duration of the war, but he wanted to see combat. This was thought by my family to be an act of patriotism and courage, but I think now that it was mainly the sense of adventure that moved him, Ben Ragan going alone into the swamp, the unknown. He came back home, to Thomasville, only once after this, I think. I was afraid to see him. He had been away long enough (in child time) to become a mysterious figure to me and an intrusion into the comfortable small-town routine I had settled into. But I also felt guilty about this, and after managing to not be on hand when he arrived—my grandparents lived across the street from us, so home-comings were handsomely staged—I persuaded my grandmother's maid to bake a nickel into one of her famous biscuits and to see to it that the mystery biscuit went only to him. Then one night at an odd hour I woke to hear my grandfather and mother talking in low voices in the bedroom next to mine, and my mother crying. We had received the conventional telegram from the War Office saying that my father was missing in action. We waited and hoped for months, but of course by the time the telegram had come he was not only missing but gone.

The story is that when my father graduated from Davidson College in 1932 he was unable to get a job as a journalist, those being hard times, so he became a free-lance writer. My grandparents, I have since learned, were very much opposed to this. They wanted him to become a lawyer, as my grandfather had been, but it is hard to imagine that they really believed he could or should be. For all of the genteel and patrician Southernness of his background, to which Davidson was no doubt intended to put the finishing touches, I think that there was a willful, renegade streak in his character which never broke out because he was otherwise obedient to the values of his family and because he became a success. He had one job: for two years he was an editor of *American Boy* magazine in Detroit; but he pined for home and eventually quit, so we all came back to Georgia. My only notion of free-lance writing was what he did, which seemed to me mostly to consist of his doing what he wanted to do and then writing something about it which he got paid money for. Obviously this is not the case with most writers, and I know, from knowing about other writers, and from my father's own records and letters, that free-lance writing is demanding work; it is an unpredictable and insecure way to make a living, and the pressure never lets up. But I still think that my youthful impression of the continuity between his life and his work is essentially correct, and the word *free-lance* therefore always had an odd, magical connotation for me. Certainly that and the kinds of experiences I have remembered my father and I sharing permanently distorted my perception of what adulthood would be like. I imagined maturity as simply an extension of childhood, only with more options and a bigger body. Men in the South generally relinquish their boyhood very unwillingly, and my father, I think, was no exception to that rule. Nor am I. To this day, when I am around my closest friends, all of whom are Southerners, though scattered now into various other regions, we behave together pretty much the way we would if we were twelve. I imagine at times, only half-seriously, that in that way I honor my father's influence and wishes. That same influence, real or imagined, perhaps causes me to read *Swamp Water* in what may seem to others a somewhat eccentric way.

Swamp Water was my father's first novel and with all of the paperback and movie rights entailed it made him a great deal of money, for those times. (Suddenly we had two Chryslers, a farm, a boat, and a part-time, laid back sort of man-servant.) The money must have purchased for him, and for us, more of the freedom and wider margins of experience that he craved and which in a way could be said to be *Swamp Water*'s principal theme. Again, in other words, the nature of his life and of his work had collaborated nicely and reinforced each other. I expect, too, that the success of *Swamp Water* in the long run had less to do with its exotic setting, its most obvious feature, than with the fact that it expressed values which many people shared, particularly Southerners and, more particularly, male Southerners.

Insofar as *Swamp Water* celebrates the simple virtues of male bonding it is squarely in the mainstream of American fiction that runs through *Huckleberry Finn*, for instance, as far back as the novels of James Fenimore Cooper. That tradition is so firmly entrenched that most male writers now, consciously or unconsciously, take it for granted and devote their attention to working variations on the theme. In the case of *Swamp Water* the variation is a frank celebration of wildness, both inside and outside human nature, and of the excitement and mystery of contending with it. In the book it is the men who are uniquely equipped by interest, strength, and nature to do that contending, and the women are left pretty much on the periphery, waiting alone on their front porches or in their homes in the settlement—civilization—at the edge of the swamp.

The Okefenokee Swamp is justly famous for having resisted all attempts of human technology to subdue and exploit it. The word *swamp* is misleading because it is in fact a kind of broad sluggish stream fed by many tributaries from its north and west and serves as the headwaters of both the St. Marys and the Suwannee rivers, one of which flows eventually into the Atlantic and the other into the Gulf of Mexico. In the last decade of the nineteenth century an attempt was made to drain the swamp in order to clear its timber and to reclaim its solid acreage for farmland. Giant dredges cut more than twelve miles of canals through its center; but the effort failed, largely because the swamp waters could not be made to flow a predictable course. In the next decades railways were run into the interior to get at the pine and cypress timber, but after the thickest and most accessible concentrations were cut nothing more could be taken out, and what remains of the old rails and steam-engine boilers and camp equipment is now covered densely with vegetation, or rusted away, or on show as quaint artifacts in the park. All but the northern tip, owned by a private corporation, the Okefenokee Swamp Park, is a National Wildlife Refuge; and although the swamp itself is now protected, the families who lived self-sufficiently in harmony with it for generations have been driven out. What one may see now on the guided tours around the fringes is only an anemic facsimile of the 680 square miles of wilderness that thrive within. This surviving wilderness and its indifference to what we ordinarily value as human is not just the setting for *Swamp Water;* what it represents in the novel and in the world is what *Swamp Water* is about.

Tom Keefer is the truly remarkable character in the book, and it is no accident that he is also the character who is most like the swamp itself, adapted to it because he is by nature wild. In the movie version he is sentimentalized, an innocent, framed victim yearning to return to care for his beautiful and innocent daughter. In the book he is unapologetically a hog-stealer and a murderer. He stole hogs, he tells Ben, from "just plain meanness. . . . Hit was sort of like hunting. I could have stole all the range hogs I wanted, but I got my enjoyment out of slipping right onto somebody's place, with yard dogs sleeping under the house, and coming out with a fat shote and not nobody catching me." His killing his sister's husband is premeditated, and he remains uncontrite. (The menfolk in town, in fact, more or less approve of the murder once they learn the facts of the case: but killing a bad man is one thing and stealing a man's hogs is another. Property values are where the community draws the line.) He can hold a live coal in his hand, without flinching, until it cools. He lives comfortably in the winter in his sparse buckskins. Ben brings him some breeches, but he declines them: "I can stay warm, if I just put my mind to it." An animal without breeches in effect does the same thing. He survives a cotton-mouth bite in his cheek by going into himself and waiting it out. He believes that animals have souls as much as men do: "[The Lord] gives folks a life, and dogs a life, and flies a life, and I don't believe He said to the dog, 'now thisn I'm a-giving you ain't good fer but a while, and when you git shed of it, you ain't got no comeback, you're just plain dead.'" He stalks and kills deer without a weapon. One of these he releases—in one of the novel's memorable scenes—after holding him in a strange, almost erotic embrace: "Sometimes I git thataway," he says to Ben, who is indignant that he has let the animal go. "When I don't need the meat, just seems like it's hard to do. Every time I grab one like that, and hold him tight up to me, and feel the life pounding and fighting in him, I just ain't got the heart." To Ben, on the other hand, "that was a dollar and a half worth of buckskin you had a-holt of." (Ben, on the whole, is not a very reflective character.) Keefer is otherwise no more sentimental about the swamp than one of its 'gators might be. It is his natural habitat, and it is getting involved with Ben in the business of trapping and of selling hides and then dreaming of going to Florida and finding a good woman and settling down that spell his doom. Others warn Ben about going *into* the swamp. Going *out* of the swamp, breaking with its natural rhythm, is what is fatal to Tom Keefer.

None of the men on the outside is like him except that by virtue of their being men, Keefer is a kind of unacknowledged model of what they all seem to dream of being. Their closest relationships are not with their wives and sweethearts but with their other male friends and their dogs. Ben's dog is honored for his headlongness and bravery by the name Trouble, and Ben is going back into the swamp to give Trouble to Tom Keefer, to whom in spirit Trouble truly belongs, when he finds Keefer dying. The hunting that the men do is ritualistic in that the dogs do the hunting and the men listen. In the night they listen to the hounds baying, drinking moonshine whisky and solemnly appreciating the nuances of nature taking her course. (The bad men, the Dorset boys, shoot nesting egrets to sell their plumes.) The men seem to be not even remotely curious about what their womenfolk might be finding to do while they are out carousing and hunting. Ben is indignant when Mabel justifiably complains that she can't be expected to just sit around and wait for him to turn up occasionally. Thursday Ragan seems to feel that Hannah's proper role is to keep him fed and otherwise to sit patiently at home alone. The marriages in the book are all bad models in one way or the other—Thursday's and Hannah's in the present, Katie's (Tom Keefer's sister) and Josiah Wicks's in the past, and Tom Keefer's dreamed-of marriage in the future. Women and marriage, in short, are on the wrong side in *Swamp Water*, standing as they do for responsibility, domestication, growing up: the opposite, in effect, of what the swamp stands for. Hannah and Thursday, it is true, are reconciled in the end, but there appears to be no reason for that other than the fact that Thursday and Ben, the men, have been reconciled. And Ben, of course, falls in love again (a "half-drunk" kind of feeling) after generalizing from Mabel's treachery that women are like cats, "pretty and soft, but you should never forget they had claws"; yet even when it is (not very convincingly) clear that

Julie and Ben are meant for each other, he seems happiest thinking that he and Thursday, now united again, can go trapping together in the swamp.

The novel's remarkable last words, spoken by Tom Keefer, are the purest expression of its spirit. The novel at the end really goes off into two different directions at once. One is toward a conventional closure: justice achieved; social stability and normalness restored. The other is quite the opposite, with Tom Keefer going into himself savoring one more adventure. It is toward him that our real sympathies are drawn: everyone else is settling down; Tom Keefer is pressing on. Normally one can tell in any serious novel where the writer's true sympathies lie—as opposed to the expected ones—simply from the degree of conviction with which the relevant characters and incidents are presented. In this case it seems to me—though, as I say my judgment is affected by my circumstances—that although the author's bias may be ambivalent, it is ultimately clear.

VEREEN BELL, JR.

PART I

BONNETS whispered against the side of the boat, loud in the black night. The little frogs peeped, and a wildcat scratched the bark of a titi tree and yowled. Ben poled silently, taking care not to rap the boat with the stob pole. Panting excitedly, the hound, Trouble, lay in the front of the boat.

Somewhere on the bank, a monkey-faced owl rolled his deep gutturals. Then, near by, came a drawn-out hiss, an ominous, chilling sound. Ben stopped the boat. He lifted the damp sack off the fire bucket, and stirred the embers. His lightwood torch blazed, the hot pitch frying.

The light danced in the black swamp water. Darkness loomed behind the spreading circle of light. Suddenly two new fires appeared, small, fierce fires — a pair of alligator eyes. Ben eased the boat toward the glowing eyes. They were wide apart — he could have laid both hands flat between them, if he had been fool enough to want to — and he knew this was the big gator he had come to kill.

Ben reached for his loaded gun. The hound whined. Immediately the gator sank.

"You keep that big mouth shut!" Ben hissed.

Ben began gator grunting. Presently the eyes reappeared, curious, not eight feet away. Ben raised the heavy gun to his shoulder with one hand, holding as close above his left eye as he could the hot torch which lit up the gun barrel. Now he could see the blinded gator's great head, even the front legs slowly treading water. He pulled the trigger.

The sound of the shot echoed and rolled; the gator went in an incredibly swift, knifing rush to a tussock, and there rolled over and over, his belly flashing, churning the water muddy. Then he disappeared. Silence came.

Ben poled to the tussock, and began methodi-

4

cally probing the soft slough bottom with his gator hook. The iron touched something. Ben made a quick jab, and when he slowly hauled the pole up, the dead gator came with it.

He couldn't get the big gator into the boat. When he tried, the boat shipped water. Finally he managed to tow his kill to the bank. He built a fire and looked at the creature.

"You've et your last foxhound now," Ben said. Two hounds, to his father's knowledge, had been caught by this gator. But revenge wasn't entirely Ben's motive in hunting out the gator. He had been afraid his own dog, Trouble, might fall prey in crossing this slough sometime, and Ben would almost as soon have been gator-eaten himself.

For a few minutes he squatted, resting. Trouble sat near him, staring sleepily at the fire. Ben reached for a piece of lightwood, then held it motionless, listening. From afar, above the *burrumf* of the bullfrogs, came the wail of a hunting panther. Ben shoved the lightwood into the fire, and watched the pitch rise to the surface and catch.

"That panther's in Okefenokee, sure's a gun's iron," he thought, half-hypnotized by the thought of the great swamp. They said Okefenokee held danger and unspeakable terrors; and yet for Ben it was a place of weird fascination.

"I'm a-going in her," he thought, "and it won't be long off."

He rolled the gator on its back. The huge tail swung in a lazy death paroxysm, its savageness gone. A leech, black with gator blood, traveled wormlike across the leather-plated belly. Ben's blade made the first incision under the lower jaw, and the hide of the belly and sides was peeled and scraped off. The horny black hide, being worthless, was left on. When the job was done, and the gator lay obscene in his pink-white nakedness, Ben cut off the tail, which tomorrow he would drag around the house to get shut of the fleas. He would cure the hide and make a fancy bridle for the horse he hoped to have some day; and maybe too he would make a purse or something for Mabel McKenzie.

They got back into the boat and headed up the slough. He poled the boat steadily, lost in his speculations of what he would find in Okefenokee. The moon rose behind the tupelo bushes, double size, and red like a hot branding iron. Night-feeding duck streamed across it, their swift wings whispering.

Ben felt Trouble move in the boat, then heard his breath hasseling in his busy nostrils. Curious, Ben stopped poling and tried to see whatever on the dark bank the hound had scented. But he made out only the ebony outlines of palmettos. Quickly he removed the sack from the fire bucket, and got the lightwood torch going.

The firelight reached the shore, dancing back farther on the white bank. With his front feet in the water, a buck deer stood, velvet antlers up, blinking at the light. He was a fine one, to be sure! Ben reached for his gun, but Trouble had stood as much as he could. The hound loosed his deep, trombone bay, jumped spang into the water, and headed for the place where the buck had been.

"Hey, come back here, *come* here!" Ben yelled. The hound swam on, shoving so impatiently that his shoulders were out of the water, whimpering anxiously and every four or five feet letting out a full-voiced hunting cry which caromed off the water and echoed through the woods.

Trouble scrambled up the sand bar and onto the bank. Then, leaving wet tracks in the packed earth, he streaked into the darkness after the buck.

"You better have your fool self a time," Ben

7

called angrily, "cause you've come on your last gator hunt with me!"

After a little while, though, Ben's anger passed and he grinned. He thought, proudly, "They's *one* buck deer in these here woods that's got a cold-out night of hauling tail ahead of him," for Trouble was known to be far-gone the best hound on the upper Suwannee River. He was a big red-and-white dog that Ben had raised from a puppy. Ben often suspected that Trouble had bird-dog blood in him, because his hindquarters were rangy like a pointer's, and whenever he scented quail or wild turkeys you could always tell it, although he didn't exactly point. He wasn't a handsome dog, his head being too big, and Thursday Ragan, Ben's father, said Trouble's tail curled so far forward over his back his hind feet were off the ground. Trouble would run with Thursday's foxhound pack, too, and stay right up front, unless he happened to run across a deer trail.

When Ben got to the place where he kept his boat, he unloaded, tossing the gator hide far up on the bank. Occasionally he would stop and listen to Trouble's ever-fainter music. "Run, deer, run," he said.

When the dog's hunting cry had faded Ben

slung the hide and tail over his shoulder, and started home, four miles away. The moon had risen higher, casting checkered blue phantoms along the trail ahead. A coon scuttled away, rattling the dry leaves.

It was nights like this Ben wished he could sing. Going home at night, with the wild woods all around him and the moon riding fancy, it would be mighty fine just to open your mouth and let the music flood out. The way Jesse Wick could, now. Jesse could just amble along, lazylike, singing away like he was the only person in the whole world, and coaxing unaccountably soft music out of his old guitar. Some said Jesse always sang at night because he was scared. But Ben thought a man that could sing like that would just naturally have to. Jesse knew all kinds of songs, a good half of them not for womenfolks' ears.

The trouble was, there were too all-fired many things a man wanted in this world, most of which he never got. Just the same, when he started trapping regular, he'd have money to buy him a guitar. That wasn't all, either. He'd have a fine young horse, about half-wild, that would go cakewalking along sideways, throwing lather, and scaring folks off the road. And he'd have him six or seven

9

more hounds like Trouble, only better about staying in a gator-hunting boat. Maybe he'd marry Mabel McKenzie; and then he'd be his own man for sure, and wouldn't have to take anything else off of his father.

It was after daylight when Ben awoke, and his father and Ford, the hired man, were plowing the cotton. He stood at the window, watching the two little brown clouds of dust that followed the men across, rolling up out of the green expanse like dry gas out of the sea. Thursday walked erect, plowing as if it were a simple chore to get done, shouting derisive things at the mule, pausing at the end of each furrow to look for fox tracks along the rail fence. The hired man plowed wearily, plodding. Ford was a young man in years, but Thursday Ragan could outplow him.

A knock sounded quietly on the door. "Ben? You woke up yet?"

"Yes'm," he said, tying his brogans.

Hannah Ragan, Thursday's young second wife, came in, her hands red from dishwashing, a mustache of fine sweat across her lip. She was about thirty, a bright-skinned woman with purplish-black hair and an easy roundness of body.

"You gitting to where you got to sleep all day," she said.

"Yes'm, but I'm my own man, now, since I'm a-paying my found."

"Gitting where you talk mighty biggety about being your own man," she observed.

"Ain't seen Trouble around nowhere, have you?"

"Sure ain't," Hannah said, turning. "Come on, Ben. The grits ought to be warmed up by now, and your ham'll be ready right off."

"I guess the old fool is still buck chasing," Ben said, following her. "He jumped spang into that gator hole and swum acrost to git at that deer."

"My," Hannah said.

Out back, the foxhounds started up a racket. Hannah looked around angrily. "Them dogs!"

Thursday's heavy foot sounded on the back porch. He came into the hall, wiping his face with his red bandanna. His blue shirt was wet halfway down his great chest, and his face was heat-reddened. He put an arm around Ben's shoulder. Ben pulled away sullenly.

"Where you been at?"

"Off," said Ben shortly.

Thursday frowned. "You heard me."

"Off gator hunting, then. I killed that hound-eating gator."

"Is that right?"

"See if that rolled-up something out yonder won't go for a gator hide."

Thursday went out. When he came back, he said, "Be dog if he won't a grandpappy. I'm sure glad he's shed of. What went with Trouble?"

"I guess he's plumb to Okefenokee by now. That's where he was headed, last time I heered him." Ben poured gravy over his grits impatiently.

"He jumped a deer?"

"Yes."

Thursday drank from the water-bucket gourd and sat down interestedly. "You see any fox sign anywheres?"

"How could I, and it dark?"

Thursday looked out the window at the sky. "Going to be powerful dry tonight if it don't dew up heavy."

Hannah's ebony eyes watched him. "I guess y'all got a fox race tonight."

Neither of them answered.

"Someday another," Hannah said, "I'll pizen them hounds."

"They's a special hot seat in hell for dog-pizeners," Thursday answered.

"Hit's there I'll be a-sitting, then," Hannah snapped. "It ain't no pleasure to stay here by myself, Thursday, and wait for you to come home from sitting on a hill drinking whisky and spitting in the fire and sayin' *Listen yonder, I believe old July done cut acrost on him.*"

"I been doing it since I was big enough to stay awake to listen," Thursday said.

"Then you ought to have a good bait of it, after fifty or sixty years." She said this with satisfaction, pointedly exaggerating Thursday's age.

"No, I ain't got quite a bait of it yet," Thursday answered ominously.

"You might git bit by a rattler."

"Might git bit in that cottonfield, but I don't see you trying to put a stop to my plowing."

"I git lonesome, Thursday."

"I told you your sister could come live with us."

"It ain't my sister I'm lonesome fer," Hannah said, looking at him.

Thursday smiled. "Couldn't be no old man you're lonesome fer."

"You ain't no old man," she said, putting her hand on his huge arm.

After dinner they hitched the mules, Kate and Sally, to the wagon and rode to the store for Saturday buying. Ben and Thursday sat on the seat, studying an occasional neighbor's crop, watching the sky, stopping sometimes to look at deer or fox tracks.

"Wisht the old fool would be back when we come home," Ben said, worriedly. "May be he's wild-hog-et by now."

"Trouble'll turn up tonight or tomorrow," Thursday said confidently. "When he hears that foxhound music a-rolling around the country tonight, he'll come in and enjoy it with 'em."

"If he's been a-running since last night, he's too God far away to hear the biggest-mouth fox dog in the world," Ben said.

Hannah didn't talk. She sat motionlessly in the cowhide chair, listening sullenly, sometimes absently admiring the jessamine and smilax that entwined the wild cherry trees. Once a pair of bobwhite quail boomed up from a near bull-grass clump and volplaned deep into the wood, weaving and tilting through the scrub oaks.

"If he ain't back by sunup tomorrow," Ben said, "I'm cold going at him."

Martin's store was crowded, as it rarely was, and wagons stood in the grove behind. Some of the mules had been unhitched; they ate their hay indifferently, waving their tails at the flies.

"Where you want to meet at tonight?" Hardy Ragan said. This younger brother of Thursday Ragan's was the adventurer of the family; he had worked in Jacksonville, and he had been to sea. He wasn't as big as Thursday, but he was built on the same scale and his red-bearded jaw had the same lean hardness.

"Thought we might try across Yellow Branch. Fiskus's boy said they's foxes yapping fit to deefen you, and Mrs. Milton said they got three of her chickens last week," Thursday said. "Gimme a snifter of that what you got on your breath."

They went to the back of the store, and Hardy drew out a bottle of homemade whisky. Thursday took a big pull at the bottle, and handed it to Ben. Ben drank, and wiped his mouth on his blue shirt sleeve. Before long, the Dorson brothers came in with their feathers.

They were little men, the two Dorson brothers, with an incredible amount of courage and an equal amount of viciousness. Silas, the one with the harelip, spread the plumes on the worn pine counter and grinned at Ben. Martin looked at the array of plumes and whistled.

"Me and Bud found us a rookery," Silas said. Ben stared at him, fascinated by the split lip and the tooth and section of red gum that it exposed.

"Where?" Ben asked automatically.

Bud said, "Down here a piece."

"Shucks," Ben said, derisively. "Ain't no call to be close-mouthed about your old rookery. You know you-all never left nothing alive in it."

"That's just about the truth," Bud Dorson said, as if Ben had paid him a compliment. "You done any good?"

"Some." Ben pointed to the hides Martin had just credited him with. The Dorson brothers looked at the coon hides, then back at him.

"I bet he's been in that Okefenokee Swamp," Silas said slowly, accusingly.

"He shore has," Bud Dorson agreed. "He God shore has."

They studied him with open jealousy and a touch of admiration.

"No I ain't," Ben said, "not yet."

"When you go," Silas said, grinning tentatively, so that the harelip spread open, "me and Bud's a-going too."

"I ain't scared of nothing that's a-living, no man ner varmints in this world, but I ain't aiming to go in that swamp and lost myself," Bud said. "Silas, my tongue's dusty as a 'bacco furrow."

"Give us a bottle, Martin!" Silas said. He turned back to Ben. "Our knees'll be a-buckling, the way we goan be loaded with plumes, a-coming out o' that swamp."

"I expect I'll go in right by myself," Ben said.

Silas's eyes darkened. "That ain't no way to do," he said.

"He's done been in there," Bud accused.

Silas patted Ben's shoulder. "He ain't been in there, Bud, not if he said he ain't. When he goes, he's goan take us. We've done told 'im we'd go, and he ain't goan turn us down. Martin, where's that whisky?"

"Come on, Martin, me and Silas and Ben Ragan is dry!"

Martin left what he was doing and handed them a bottle of red whisky. Silas opened it, eagerly. Bud reached for it. The bottle slipped and struck the floor, and broke, the liquid spreading darkly over the tobacco-spit-stained boards. Immediately Silas and Bud, cursing, fell to their bellies on the floor and began licking at the whisky, trying to pool it up with their hands, pushing the broken pieces of glass away from their tongues.

Ben went outside. Mabel McKenzie was standing beside their wagon, talking to Hannah. Her glossy black hair was pulled down tight behind her head. She smiled at Ben possessively.

"Howdy," Ben said.

"What's all the hollering in yonder about?" Mabel asked.

"The Dorson boys spilled some whisky," Ben said.

"Hit's gitting where a lady cain't come on Saturday, even in the middle of the afternoon," Mabel complained.

Hannah said, "Ain't it so?"

Ben, ill-at-ease, walked up front to have a look at the mules.

"I guess you heered about the sing," Mabel said.

Ben rubbed Kate's nose. "Seem like I did."

Mabel said, "I'll fix us up a nice dinner."

Ben hesitated, rebelling at Mabel's assurance. *Sometimes she acts purely bossified,* he thought.

"I may not be here," he said.

"Where you think you'll be at?" Hannah asked.

"Ain't no telling."

"You cain't just pure-out miss the sing," Mabel said.

"I may not be here."

"Well," Mabel said coldly, "you can do just like you please."

"I may be in Okefenokee Swamp. Ain't no telling."

Mabel's mouth opened. "Don't you go in that place, Ben!"

"He ain't going in there," Hannah smiled. "He's just sort of big-mouthed lately."

"Well," Mabel said, "you let me know about the sing." She spoke with an ominous indifference.

"I may be able to make it," he said.

"Hit really don't make much difference, neither way."

"I expect I'll be there," Ben admitted.

"You didn't mean it about the swamp, I don't reckon."

"Well, maybe I did, and maybe I didn't. If old Trouble ain't come back before long, I got him to go look fer, and I reckon the swamp's where I better head."

The hound had long since ceased baying, now running silently in an even-paced lope. Occasionally he found places where the deer had rested, leaving hot scent lying like a miasma in the palmetto thickets.

The deer stayed on the highest bits of land, it seemed; possibly because on the bank of every slough and black-water run the alligators lay basking in the bubbling sun, and in the water they moved like charred logs; and in the green maiden cane that bordered the water great cottonmouths five feet long, and big around as a cypress sapling, waited in lazy half-sleep. Once a fawn joined the buck, and they ran together, unhurriedly, for several miles. When they had crossed the island, they swam. Suddenly there was a swift rush of water. The fawn let out a terrified bleat that ended in a watery gurgle, and then on the surface there was a mild boiling and the flick of a leathery tail.

After a while, the buck stopped and nibbled at some huckleberry bushes. Then he lay down in a great patch of live-oak shade and rested. For a long time he kept his head up, his tan ears turning this way and that, his nostrils twitching. The only sounds were bird and insect sounds: the hum of bees in a hollow cypress, the crescendo rasp of the locusts, the wild imperious cackle of an ivory-billed woodpecker, flying high over the treetops with white bill shining, the chuckle of the herons, the scolding of a tiny wren that danced on a fallen bay tree.

Some time later, horribly close by, there was a triumphant bell-like hound cry. In terror the deer sprang up in a fifteen-foot leap, and the dog Trouble ran in a blind rush, straining to reach the furiously flexing hams. The deer struck the water and Trouble was beside him, swimming powerfully. Trouble tried to seize the buck's ear. To avoid him, the buck pulled his head to one side, and they swam in circles in the black water. Trouble got the ear in a savage, snapper-turtle hold. The deer, now swimming not very strongly for the opposite bank, tried to hook the dog off with his sensitive velvet antlers. The deer swam slowly, sometimes hardly moving, hooking sideways at the dog. Eventually they reached the other bank. The deer pulled himself out of the water, then tried to turn and get the dog in front of him; but instead he fell, and the dog, still holding the ear, fell with him. They lay helpless, both too exhausted to get up.

The fox hunters had a little fire going, not because they needed its warmth, but to have something to stare at, and spit at, and light pipes at. The dogs were away but silent.

Hardy Ragan said, "Hit were like shooting cows, Grandpa said. They was barge after barge of them. They was close to three hund'rd Britishers, and they won't but thirty fellows with Captain Cone."

"What was them British wanting to git to Trader's Hill fer?" Ben asked.

Fiskus, the blind fiddler, sat back, a little away from the others, played light, low notes, his fiddle against his chest. Ben turned over, brushing the pebbles away. One of them fell flat. Ben held it up toward the dim light of the fire. An arrowhead; flint, with serrated edges.

Hardy took a pull at the whisky jug, leaning to the fire, and you could see his red beard and the brown hair that lay on the back of his neck. "They was going up the St. Mary's to wreck Major Clark's sawmill — Trader's Hill were some place in 1812. They'd just nick them British off from the tupelo bushes on the bank, and then run around a bend and shoot again, and then run around the next bend and shoot some more. Finally them British come to they senses and give it up, and started back down. Grandpa and them just turned around and went back down too, shooting right on. They was a hund'rd and fifty of them British killed, and nair one of Cone's bunch got the first mortal lick."

Far off, the high-pitched yelp of a young hound sounded twice. They listened.

"Turkey thought he had run up on something," Fiskus said mildly, still playing soft, light notes.

"Look a-here at this arrowhead I found," Ben said presently.

They passed it around, looking at it indifferently. "That ain't no Seminole," Thursday said.

"Creek," said Hardy. "She's old-timey. The red-tail that shot thisn's got a fifty-year cypress growing over 'im. When Gen'l Charley Floyd went into the swamp, they wasn't but mighty few bows and arrows found. Them son-of-a-guns had rifles and shotguns, from wheel-locks to cap-and-ball."

"Stole 'uns, I reckon," somebody said.

"My pa said there never was nobody like the Indians fer stealing. A hog ner cow wasn't to be trusted out, till Gen'l Floyd run them scoun'ls to Florida."

Thursday said, "Don't guess your pa never knowed Tom Keefer."

"You reckon where that rascal went at?"

Hardy said, "Savannah, er Jacksonville, I imagine. You can catch onto a boat, like I did, and won't nobody never git up with you."

"Well, he better not never come back here."

Ben sat up and spat at the fire, thoughtfully. It was over a year, now, since Keefer killed Josiah Wick and disappeared. The way Ben remembered it, Tom said Josiah had got to beating his wife, who was Tom's sister; and to tell the truth, she did have a bruised-up face the day after the killing. But she said Josiah hadn't ever beat her, that she fell down in the smokehouse and hurt herself. She said Josiah caught Tom stealing a shote, and that was how come Tom killed him. So after his own sister said that, the next thing anybody knew, Tom was gone. He was the slickest thief ever known of around there, so excepting hanging for murdering Josiah Wick, being shut of him for good was the next best thing.

A distant, tentative baying came to them. Then it increased, became frenzied, and was presently joined by the deeper voices of the pack.

"Here we go!" one of the men shouted. "That was Fiskus's dog Turkey."

"Old Turkey's a real dog," Thursday said. "My Sadie was right in there, too."

The pack was singing now, the song rolling up

24

the hill to the listeners, and they could imagine the little gray wraith that ran like a shadow before the dogs, cutting back, double-crossing, climbing trees and jumping branches; crafty, devilish.

Ben listened to the assorted voices of the pack, each of them easily identifiable to all who sat on the hill. Ben waited for the clear basso of Trouble to join in; tired, hungry Trouble, back from chasing a buck deer clean to Okefenokee before giving him up. Ben listened so hard he could almost hear Trouble, sure enough. But not quite. *Before long,* he thought with a sick uneasiness, *I got him to go git.*

Blind Fiskus laid his fiddle down for a moment, and turned his face toward the fire, holding his head back, nostrils dilating. Then he got up and walked straight to the whisky jug. When he finished he came back to his fiddle and held it quiet under his arm, listening to distant, sweeter music.

Hannah sat on the porch in the thick shadow of the wisteria vine with its fading, sugar-sweet lavender blossoms. So distant you couldn't be sure about hearing it, she listened to the hounds, hating their voices. She folded her arms under her full breasts. She rocked gently, lonesomely.

They had warned her against marrying a man as old as Thursday, but she wouldn't listen. She hadn't expected him to take on over her like a young lover with hardly a fuzz on his jaw. But it would have been all right except for the hounds. It wasn't an old man they needed to have warned her about, it was a fox-hunting old man.

Abruptly she sat still, listening. Someone was coming along the road. A tremor went over her, and suddenly she was frightened, a strange new feeling for her.

Then she made out the sounds that came down the road to her, and relaxed. Somebody was singing, and playing a guitar as he walked.

> "*Come here, little wife,*
> *And explain this thing to me.*
> *Whose head is that beside you*
> *Where my head ought to be?*
>
> "*You blind fool, you crazy fool,*
> *It looks like you could see*
> *It's only a cabbage head*
> *My mamma brought to me.*

"I've traveled this world over
A hundred times or more,
But a cabbage head with whiskers
I never seen before."

The voice was Jesse Wick's. Hannah listened as his fingers strummed absent-minded chords on the guitar. He was always singing and playing that way.

Hannah didn't know whether to speak to him or not. Finally she decided she'd better, because Jesse seemed not to realize he was passing somebody's house, and no telling what kind of song he might sing next.

"Evening, Jesse," she said clearly.

Jesse Wick stopped playing and was silent for a moment, and she knew she had startled him.

"Ma'am?" he called. "That you, Miss Hannah?"

"Yes. I heard you playing."

"You'll have to excuse me. It didn't come to mind I was near nobody's place."

"Hit's all right."

"Pretty night, ain't it?"

"Terrible pretty."

"How you coming, Thursday?" Jesse called.

"He ain't here. Just me. He's a-hunting."

Jesse was silent for a moment. "I recollect hearing the dogs a while back, now that you speak on it." He waited a moment before he went on. "You right by yourself?"

"Ford's down in the barn, 'sleep."

Jesse said nothing. She could hear the guitar strings vibrating. "I was enjoying it. Maybe I shouldn't of spoke and put a stop to it."

"I guess I could start it up again, easy as not," he said.

In the dimness she could see him climbing up on the gatepost to sit.

"She came slowly, slowly up
To the place where he was lying,
Then to him they heard her say,
'Young man, I think you're dying.'

" 'If I had a kiss from your precious lips
It'd keep my life from going.'
'Before you'd get a kiss from my lips
I'd see your red blood flowing.'

"He turned his face upon the wall
And death was in him dwellin',
The only words they heard him say,
'Hardhearted Barbara Ellen.'"

There just wasn't anybody who could sing like Jesse Wick. "That's purely pretty," Hannah said.

"Never had to balunst on no gatepost to sing before," Jesse laughed.

Hannah hesitated. "You could set on the porch."

"Don't care if I do," he said, and climbed down, singing softly, " *'Go put up your horses and give them some hay, come set down here beside me, as long as you can stay.' 'My horses they ain't hungry and they won't eat your hay; my wagon it's done loaded and I'm going on my way.'* "

After a while, Jesse said, "Didn't figure to have no enjoymint like this when I started out."

She looked over to the steps, where he sat. "Hit's been sort of nice. I take to music, specially when I git sort of lonesome." She rose, uncertainly. "Reckon I better be gitting on to bed."

"You reckon you had?"

"I expect so."

"I'm just gitting warmed up."

"I better go on in, I reckon."

"Well, I'll be coming back," Jesse said.

Hannah didn't answer.

"Next time I hear them hounds a-hunting," Jesse said, "I'll be back."

*　*　*

Outside, day was breaking as Ben hurriedly ate breakfast. Thursday was overly attentive to Hannah, as he always was on mornings after a fox race.

"Look at her," he said, "her cheeks is the color o' peaches. I swear, Hannah, you're a right pretty woman."

She served his coffee nervously. "You catch air fox?"

"You know we caught air fox. One old scoun'l run them dogs fer an hour before he treed. Then Ben clumb up and shuck him out, and be dog if he didn't run 'em another half an hour. That were shore a fine race."

Ben stood up. He went back of the stove and got a flour sack and began putting things in it.

"You done?" Hannah said.

"My dog ain't back. I'm going at him," Ben said.

"You be careful, son," Thursday warned.

Ben filled a bottle with matches, stoppered it, and didn't answer.

"When you coming back?" Hannah asked.

"When I find that fool hound dog. It may be a day and it may be a month," he said.

Thursday said, firmly, "You be back here by tomorrow night."

"You know I cain't find that dog right off the bat."

"You be back here by tomorrow night," Thursday said, "er not a-tall."

"I got to git that dog."

"You heard me, I reckon."

Hannah said, "You ain't never been that hardminded at him before, Thursday."

"He ain't never headed for that swamp before neither."

"If he was your dog, you'd go at him," Ben said.

"I reckon you heard me."

"I'll try to git back by then."

"Don't try. Git back."

"If that's the way you want to act," Ben said stubbornly, "I don't care where I git back er no."

"That's plumb up to you."

Ben went into his room and got his barlow knife and a blanket and clothes. When he came out, he kissed Hannah on the cheek.

"Good-by, Miss Hannah."

"You try to git back, Ben, like he says," she whispered.

Ben shouldered his bundle, slung his horn around his neck, and walked out, holding his gun in his left hand, his jaw muscles bunched angrily.

* * *

The swamp, with its morasses, and jungle growths so thick they said you had to back up to bat your eyes, wasn't easily invaded. But the swamp was full of water, slow-flowing water; and this had to come out somewhere. So Ben paddled steadily up the black little Suwannee River.

Every hour or so he stopped to blow the cow horn that was slung with a piece of rawhide around his neck, then to listen for the far-off answering bay of a lost hound dog. The sound startled the cat squirrels that frolicked in the tupelo trees, and once brought to the surface a big alligator turtle with its corrugated shell and malignant stare. A joree ran along the leaf-littered sandbank, chirping with absent-minded friendliness and twisting his black-hooded head.

The sun rode high. Ben went ashore and unwrapped his ham-and-biscuit lunch, and ate, squatting by the water's edge and watching the redbellies that rose with popping mouths to take his crumbs. When he had finished, he blew the horn some more, and listened, stock-still, but no sound came back except the scream of a fish eagle.

Again he paddled, now beginning to feel doubtful about the wisdom of following the river. After a while, though, the firm sandbanks sank and became low muck, bordered with lush green maiden cane. Instead of tupelo bushes there were runty bays, and titi bushes, and paintroot. Ahead rose tall trees — the tallest he had ever seen. The boat was entering a long, narrow lake, and he knew he was in the swamp. The wild majesty of it caught at his throat.

On the left side of the lake were the cypresses, taller than highland pines, savagely graceful from their wet swollen boles to their slim tops with distant greener-than-grass foliage and graybeard moss, gently waving. There was row after row of them, as far as the eye could see, each of them kingly, casting their green shadows into the still, bonnet-covered water. Hundreds of wood ducks flew about in them, squealing, lighting on the slender branches, their thin cries echoing throughout the vast green cathedral. A poor-joe bird rose in agitation, squawling indignantly back at the boatman.

On the right side of the lake was a jungle wall of many colors, of bright bay and amber berries and yellow jessamine and scarlet ivy trumpets and pink hurrah blossoms. The white of the Cherokee roses was spattered everywhere. He paddled on, uneasily. The gators in the lake watched him curiously. They sank before his boat, and presently came up behind it, hissing. Once he brought up a two-foot gator on his paddle blade.

Three half-grown bears in a bee tree stopped their busy work to regard the visitor, raising their noses high to catch scent of him. A huge cottonmouth, big around as a man's neck, lay near the boat, rocking gently in the undulating water, and watching Ben with a stare of cold hate. Its tongue licked in and out like live rubber. Ben swung the paddle against the flat, evil head. "Git!" he said, and the snake fled in zigzag alarm into the dense water grass.

The wood ducks were quiet now, and a weird hush fell over the swamp. The silence grew, like a dumb monster watching solemnly from the cypresses. Ben shivered. He struck the side of the boat with the paddle, just to hear a noise, but even that sound seemed smothered.

This'd be a ideal time to give a good hard blow on the horn, while everything's so unnatural quiet. He raised the cool horn to his mouth, then hesitated, his animal instincts warning him not to make his presence conspicuous. But how would he find Trouble if he didn't blow the horn?

Finally, he blew. The sound was incredibly

loud, echoing and re-echoing, until the sky was full of startled birds, ducks and limpkins and bitterns and ibises. They disappeared, and again the silence came, broken only by something like the faint far-off honking of a wild goose.

Ben jumped. The wild-goose sound was a distant dog's baying. Excitedly he blew the horn again, and presently the answer came again, floating thinly to him, then suddenly breaking off. He blew the horn repeatedly, and got no further answer. But now he had the direction. He started paddling.

The lake narrowed, became shallow. Ben changed from paddle to pole, and sent the boat through the black water, rustling against the lily pads. On one side of the narrow run the thicket persisted. On the other now the cypresses were gone, and instead there was a vast bogland of half-petrified logs and charred stumps and stagnant water. Ben figured that Trouble had been obliged to go through the thicket at one time or another. Perhaps, by going on all fours, he himself could get through.

He shoved the boat under the bushes to the bank, and stepped out onto the semisolid earth. At the weight of his step, bushes thirty feet away

3 5

trembled. On his knees, he saw a small opening, a tunnel through the low bushes of the thicket. He squeezed into it, and wriggled his way along for several feet. The thorns fought at him, and the muscular vines seemed deliberately to entwine his hands and feet.

Abruptly he heard a noise, and at the same time he noticed that the ground beneath him was wavering, like a gentle ocean swell. Coming toward him in the tunnel was a big gator, running with his flat head parallel to the ground, his great jaw agape so that Ben could see the yellow stoblike teeth and beefy tongue. Before Ben could think at all, the monster was at him, and Ben instinctively rolled sidewise, pressing his body hard into the matted vines and thorns. The claws of the gator's hurrying back foot raked against his thigh, ripping the denim trousers. Then there was a splash outside somewhere, and silence.

Trembling, Ben turned around and headed out. *Might meet another old son of a gun that don't want to be cut off from the water.*

Two hundred yards farther on, he found an opening in the thicket, and through it he could see high land — palmetto clumps and a pine forest. He looked at the sun — halfway down. He shoved his boat up on the bank and got out.

Gun under his arm, he stepped through the opening in the thicket. There was a quick movement somewhere near him. Ben whirled, and met a brilliant, abrupt shattering of consciousness.

It was almost dusk when Ben opened his eyes. His hands were tied behind him tightly; his back was against an oak sapling. A fire flickered around a blackened pot. Beyond stood a rough palmetto-roof shelter; to one of its cabbage-palm supports was tied the hound, Trouble, who lay quietly panting, watching Ben. A big buck deer hung between two live oaks, its skin in places loose and wrinkled, as if it had been rolled back to expose the saddle meat.

The man stood down near the water's edge, a tall alert figure in a rough-cut buckskin shirt and short buckskin trousers that were hardly trousers at all; barefooted. He was so dark Ben at first thought he was an Indian. His beard was thin, and in tufts, a spot of it on each jaw, another on his chin. The man came back to the fire, walking absolutely without sound, almost as if he were not actually touching the earth; but his steps were springy, exuberant. His legs were very long and hard and knotty; his knees bulged, like two apples in a pair of stockings. There was no one else; it was a one-man camp.

Ben's head throbbed; his eyeballs moved in little puddles of pain, and he seemed to hear his eyelids open and close, as if they were paper. A thick matting of dried blood and hair covered the aching back of his head.

Ben watched the man stirring the pot, almost too sick to be interested. He wouldn't have believed any living thing could have got as close to him, without his knowing it, as the man must have been.

"If you've done hurt that dog," Ben said, "you damn shore better be careful how you untie me from here!"

The man came to him. "Thought once I might've knocked your brains clean out, the way you done," he said. "That dog's all right, less'n a full belly is bad for him."

Ben flexed his wrists. "How come you give me that lick on the head?"

The man went back to the fire, inspecting the big pot, and then the smaller earthen one in the embers. He took an absorbed interest in the cooking. He would squat there motionlessly, like some sort of bony, graceful animal, then in that springy step move around to the other side, and squat again, watching.

"Hit's a long time since I tasted coffee. My God, hit smells good. When I found it in your boat, I et a handful of grounds."

Ben said, slowly, "We was wondering, the other night, what ever went with you."

The man looked down his shoulder at him, sharply. "Did you come at me?"

"I come at my dog, that's all."

Tom Keefer squatted in silence, staring thoughtfully into the fire, his mind no longer on the coffee. Finally he ate, and fed Trouble. Then he began sharpening his hunting knife, slowly and carefully.

"Bud, I'm mighty sorry you turnt out to know me," Keefer said.

Ben watched the knife. The blade shone, the thin red light from the fire dancing along the edge like blood.

"If you was to let me take my dog and go, I'd promise not to tell it on you about hiding in Oke-fenokee," Ben suggested.

"I don't expect I could do that," Keefer told

3 9

him. He wiped the knife clean, and looked at Ben appraisingly, as at a hog about to be butchered.

Chill sweat stood on Ben's upper lip. *Father, let him do it with a quick lick.*

An hour passed.

Still Tom Keefer delayed, cutting little pieces of bark off to test the knife edge. He went down to the water's edge and drank, his long, angular frame flat on the black wet muck. When he came back, he again sharpened the knife, with painful deliberation.

Tom Keefer muttered, "I can still see that other fellow flopping around and thumping on the floor boards, see him like it was last night, and he God shore needed killing. What you reckon I'll have on my mind from now on, when the owls is chuckling and gators is noisy and I cain't git to sleep?" Finally he shoved his knife into its wild-hog-hide sheath purposefully. "Well, hit won't be no boy with a cut throat on my mind."

"You ain't goan do it?"

"No, I ain't."

Ben was too sick to feel relief.

After a while, Keefer said, "But you're in Oke-fenokee for good, Bud. If I let you go back, you'll tell it on me, first thing."

"Not if I said I wouldn't."

"I wouldn't trust nobody. Your word don't mean nothing to me, not when my living er hanging's independent on it."

"I ain't goan stay. I'll git away sometime, if I have to bust you on the head when you ain't looking."

"Bud, when we git where we're going, they ain't but one way to find your way outn this swamp — and that's with me showing you. Maybe you don't know, but Okefenokee's a mighty big wet place. They's seven hundred square miles of it, and not no signposts ner nobody to tell you. I don't believe the man is alive that can catch me when I ain't looking, but if you was to, you'd parish to death trying to git out by yourself. I ain't just running off at the mouth; you'll see."

Ben did see. That night they moved camp. In Keefer's boat for two hours they delved deeper into the mysterious swamp, while the night was alive and ominous around them. Ben tried to keep his sense of direction, but finally he gave up; the swamp all looked alike. Keefer had not been lying. Only by purest luck would a man live to find his way out. But, Ben thought, that didn't matter. If he got a chance, he meant to try it.

41

In the days that followed, he learned that Keefer was more swamp animal than man. Without his ever seeming to be particularly alert, even when they were out visiting Keefer's quail and turkey traps, there was never a moment when Ben felt that he had an opportunity to attack. Keefer had of course taken the gun, and kept the ax and any other possible weapons out of Ben's reach.

If it hadn't been that he was a prisoner, the life wouldn't have been so bad. The forays for food with Trouble and Keefer occupied some of the time.

"I give out of gunpowder months ago," Keefer said. "Learned to do plumb without it. We'll save yourn till we need it to keep from gitting panther-et er something."

They were searching for a bee tree near a pond. A swamp bear appeared on the opposite side, to hunt the soft bank for turtle eggs, but he caught scent of them, and disappeared with a great crackling of brush. After a while, a small drove of wood ducks came into the pond, whimpering, and lit. The drakes moved about busily, their bright feathers and head tufts catching the morning sun.

Presently there was another movement of wings, and a large bird dropped into the water a few feet from the brush-covered shore, straightening pink feathers. For a moment then it waited motionlessly, and finally thrust its spoon-shaped bill down into the water.

"We goan have curlew for dinner," Keefer whispered. Screened by bay bushes, he crept around the edge of the pond on his belly, moving when the curlew had its head down feeding, lying immobile when its head was up. After what seemed to Ben an interminable time, Keefer was within five yards of the bird, shielded by the low brush. In his hand he held a three-foot piece of lightwood, and now, quickly, he rose and threw. The missile struck the surprised bird's head. Beating its pink wings upon the water, the curlew flopped out toward the center of the pond and then died with a feeble trembling.

Keefer shrugged out of his meager buckskin shirt and trousers, and slid into the water like an otter, and swam toward the curlew. When he came back, Ben was waiting with the sheath knife Keefer had left with his clothes. When Keefer reached the shallower water and stood up Ben jabbed the knife point hard against a long scar on the naked brown belly, and drops of blood mingled with the dripping water.

"Now's a good time to make up your mind

where you want to take me out of here peaceable," Ben said, "er have me bury this blade in your guts a little bit at the time until you decide to."

Keefer dropped the curlew. "I thought about that knife in my clothes right after I got in the water," he said.

Later, when Ben was thinking back, he figured just about what must have happened. Keefer's iron hand, all of a sudden, was clamped around Ben's wrist. At the same time, Keefer sucked his belly in, away from the knife, and before Ben could shove the blade forward against the steely grip, Keefer had slipped sideways. Keefer's hard elbow struck Ben's jaw with jolting force. As Ben fell back, Keefer snapped the arm that held the knife around behind Ben's back, and shoved upward with such savage force that Ben's fingers sprang open in sudden, agonized pain, and the knife leaped into the bay bush.

"You see there?" Keefer said, breathing easily.

"Not quite yet!" Ben said, turning quickly, dragging his arm out of Keefer's grasp, feeling the burning pain that raced through strained ligaments.

For several minutes, then, they fought. Quick

as a timber rattler, Keefer was almost impossible to hit; and, being wet and naked, hard to hold. Furthermore, those long, ropy muscles held power and what seemed to be absolute tirelessness. Just when Ben thought he was getting slightly the upper hand, he found himself on his back in the silty water, with Keefer's hard hands around his throat, and he knew he either had to quit or be immediately drowned.

Standing over him, Keefer said, "You're a good man, Bud, but you got to give it up now." He released his hold, pulled Ben upright, and stepped on the bank. "Come on."

That afternoon, Ben lay in the shade of the live oak, half sick, his strength gone like blood from his veins. Keefer pulled a fat tick from Trouble's neck, and said:

"Don't know as I ever seen a better hound dog than thisn. How come I happen to have him, I seen him and that buck deer coming acrost Billy's Lake, him onto the buck's ear, and the buck trying to hook him off. When they got to the bank, wasn't neither one of 'em could hardly move, and they just laid there, plumb give out. I killed the deer with a light'rd knot. Plenty hounds'll run a deer for you, but thisn's the first I seen that'd purely catch one and hold 'im fer you," he mused in profound admiration. He rose and stretched.

Presently he said, "Guess I'll go git a drink of swamp water."

Ben dozed.

When he woke, Keefer was bent over the pot, slowly and deliberately stirring a tea of hais-law. Keefer's left cheek was puffed and bloody, and his eyes held a curious dullness. He drank the tea and painfully arose, and stupidly, like a man with no brain, walked to his pine-straw bed and lay down.

"What's got into you?" Ben asked.

Keefer's eyes opened, but there was no light in them. He didn't answer. Finally Ben thought to follow the path to the water's edge. Half mashed into the soft muck of the bank was a dead cottonmouth moccasin, his head beaten to shapelessness. Already the blowflies were busy about it, and Ben knew that he must have been asleep for an hour or so. The prints of Keefer's big hands were in the muck, filled with water, where he had knelt to drink when the snake struck his cheek. The sheath knife lay where it had dropped after Keefer cut his cheek to bleed the wound.

Ben went back to camp and after a while he

located his gun. Then he began the search for Keefer's boat, carrying Trouble with him on a leash of rawhide.

He found the boat shoved deep into a brush-covered inlet. Three soft-shelled turtles slid off it into the water. The boat was a shallow cypress dugout; you could still see spots of blackened wood where the log had been burned and then dressed out. The stob pole floated beside the boat.

They got into the boat and started poling, heading toward the long lake that would lead them out of the swamp. *Reckon my girl's wondering what come of me.* It was the first time he had thought of Mabel McKenzie in days.

Far overhead, two buzzards wheeled slowly, almost motionless against the white clouds. Ben stood still a moment, letting the pole trail in the dying wake of the boat. He looked at the buzzards again.

"I don't expect I ought to just go right off and leave him there. Somebody ought to kind of bury him. From his looks he'll be dead by morning," he thought, uneasily.

Resolutely, he turned the boat back toward camp. Keefer lay in exactly the same position. His breathing was hardly audible. It occurred to Ben

47

that he was dying mighty easy for a man that had been cottonmouth-bit.

Before dawn, Ben rose and looked at Keefer again. He didn't touch him, but no breathing was audible. Ben began working on a makeshift grave. Daylight had come when he finished it, and he decided he better say some sort of funeral speech.

I'm going to git him, now, Lord, and put him down in it. A dead soul's a-coming, and hit ain't nobody but Tom Keefer but he died without no hollering ner cutting the fool, just like a natural man. He killed a fellow in his day, and stole many a pig, Lord. I wouldn't tell it on him, but you know it good as I do. I ain't going to hold nothing against him, not even him trying to steal old Trouble. So if you want to go sort of light on him, too, hit'll be all right with me. Amen.

Ben hesitated, then went to the camp. Tom Keefer was half sitting up, resting on his elbow, his eyes dazed.

"Never thought to see you around here no more," Keefer said slowly.

"I sort of stayed to bury you," Ben muttered. "Looks like I went to the trouble for nothing."

Keefer sat up, painfully. "If I let them things kill me, I'd a been dead a long time ago. I bet I

48

been cottonmouth-bit a dozen times," he said. "Ain't no doctors out here. I just make up my mind to git well, and think hard on it, and maybe pray some. I'll be up from here afore night."

Ben stared at him, not sure whether to be glad or sorry that Keefer was alive.

While he built the fire, Keefer watched him. "Ben," he said weakly, "you had a chancet to leave me, and you never took it. I ain't going to keep you here. When I git a little better I'll show you the way out. I know you ain't going to tell them about me, if you say you ain't."

"I ain't going to tell."

"Maybe sometime another you'll come back, and we'll have us some hunts, me and you and Trouble."

"I been thinking. They's one gracious heap of coon and otter in this here place. I could bring us some traps in here, and my God at the hides we could catch! I'd take them out to sell, and we'd split the money. Don't know what you'd want with money out here, though, come to think of it."

"I got a good use for it, if I ever git a-holt of any," Keefer said, slowly.

PART II

JESSE WICK'S fingers
were busy on the guitar strings. Even when
he talked, they went on, and the guitar gave
its mellow response. Jesse said:
"I think about old Thursday out yonder listening to them hounds, and me setting here talking to his pretty wife, and I nearly laugh out
loud."

Hannah admitted, "I git nervous-like. He
might think something."

Jesse said, "What?"

"You know."

"How come you got yourself tied up to an old man like him?"

"He ain't so old."

"He's fifty er more, ain't he?"

"Yes, but he ain't old. Just gone all the time."

"If it was me, right here's where I'd stay at," Jesse said.

She said nothing. He went on, "Hannah, I wish to God it was me."

"You know better than to talk like that."

"I wish to God it was me, just the same."

She looked away. She said, finally, "I keep worrying about Ben."

"Set down here, where I can see you."

"I imagine it's about time for me to be gitting in."

"You can set down a minute."

She sat down beside him on the steps. Occasionally, far away, came the hunting cry of hounds. She listened, and shivered. "I never reckoned Ben'd be gone two whole weeks."

Jesse shifted his guitar a little, and his arm rested against Hannah's. She moved, but when he began singing he touched her again and she didn't seem to notice.

"I'll cross that swampland one more time
If the tears don't fall and blind me,
Cross that swampland one more time
For the girl I left behind me."

"Did you ever have a girl and leave her?" Hannah asked.

"Not a shore-enough girl," he answered. "That's just an old song."

"It's right sad."

"Never seen nobody that suited me," he said, "up till now."

Hannah stirred. The guitar, for once, was silent. His hand closed on her leg, gently.

"Don't do that, Jesse," she said, her face turned to look at him.

He laid the guitar down. "Hannah, you know what I been trying to tell you."

"I guess I do, but — "

His hand touched her face, caressingly; then it grew firm under her chin, and he kissed her. She tried to draw back, but now he held her; her body gave a little toward his.

"I knowed you ain't been wanting me to stop by without caring something about me," Jesse whispered, and kissed her again.

"No," she protested, her cheek against his, "it ain't right."

He held her tightly, so that he could feel the heave of her breast against him.

She began crying. "I ain't the kind of woman to act like this."

"Ain't nothing to cry about," he said. He loosened his hold on her.

"I git lonesome, with him gone two er three times a week, and then too busy catching up on his sleep to have any time for me," she said, crying softly. "Seems like what little pleasure I git is when you come along."

"You ought not to keep a-crying like that," Jesse said. He stood up. "Maybe I better go."

"Don't go right yet."

"I expect I better," he said nervously.

She walked to the gate with him, drying her tears. "I don't guess you better come back no more, had you?"

He looked down at her face, dim in the night light. A mockingbird flew to the top of the house and sat on the lightning rod and sang. Jesse grasped her arm determinedly. "I aim to be back soon."

"Listen," she said, "somebody's a-coming."

Jesse jerked away, startled. "You reckon it's him?" he hissed.

She grasped his arm. "Wait. Don't run."

A silhouette moved toward them, the silhouette of a man and a dog, walking wearily, plodding. The dog was tied to the man's belt.

"Ben!" Hannah cried.

"Howdy, Miss Hannah," Ben grinned, hugging her. "I guess y'all give me out, didn't you?"

Jesse stood motionless, cold sweat on his upper lip.

Ben looked at him, and made out who it was. "Howdy, Jesse."

Jesse said, nervously, "I was just passing by, and she come out to ask me had I seen you."

Hannah still held Ben. "Oh, Ben! How come you stayed so long?"

"I told him I'd be back when I got ready. I just yesterday got ready."

"I knowed you was going to do that way."

Jesse said, "I just happened to be passing along, on my way home, and she come out to ask me had I seen you."

"You been in that swamp all this time, Ben?"

"Yes'm, I reckon I have," he said. "Guess I'll

git on in. Me and this damn-fool dog has traveled ourself half to death."

"I'll fix you a little something to eat."

Jesse Wick said, "I told her I hadn't seen nothing of you. Don't guess I'd been here more'n a minute when you come. Just happened to be passing by." He moved away about a yard. "Expect I'd better be a-rambling."

"Good night."

Jesse walked faster and faster, automatically holding his guitar so it wouldn't bump up and down. The moonlight threw phantoms across the road, but he was glad of the shadows. He stayed near the trees, hurrying in the darkness, his breath whistling out of his open mouth. "He'll be sure to tell him, when he comes home, first thing," he thought fiercely. He began to run.

It looks to me like you better stay home sometime, Papa, and see what's a-going on. what you mean by that, ben? *Well, you better stay and see for your own self.* what you mean, anyway? *That fellow Jesse Wick was here. I come up on him and Miss Hannah.* you mean last night. *Yes, last night I come right up on 'em. They was standing by the gate, like he was just leaving. She had a-holt of his arm.* you be careful what you say,

5 6

boy. *Well, you stay around sometime and see for yourself.* i expect he was just passing by, and stopped a minute to be neighborlike. *That's what he said but his tracks was all in the yard.* you better not be lying to me, ben. *You'd better stay home sometime and see for your own self.* i expect i better go tend to jesse wick right now. . . .

Jesse's breath came almost as loud as the pound of his running feet. A bat flitted with clicking wings down the road ahead of him. "He'd come right down this road looking for me," Jesse thought suddenly, and turned off into the wood to short-cut the way home. Now catclaw briers grabbed at him, and unseen things struck him, and he stumbled drunkenly as he ran. Then he thought: "But my house is where he'd head for, and there I'd be, laying up asleep." He even heard the explosion from Thursday's gun, and saw the blinding flash, then in terrified fascination he watched himself roll spasmodically out of the bed to the floor, the way Sarah Wick said his brother, Josiah, had done when Tom Keefer killed him. A cypress knee struck his foot, and he fell, the guitar glancing off a stump with an abrupt *bong*.

Jesse went back toward the road. When he reached it, he stopped behind an elderberry bush,

5 7

trying to hold his breath so he could listen. The night was quiet; no one was coming. He stepped into the road and ran again. Presently he reached the creek bridge. He slid down the black-mud embankment and crept into the darkness under the bridge. A small frog yipped and dived with a tiny splash into the warm, slow-flowing creek. Jesse lay on his stomach on the cool earth. One arm was cramped under him, the way he had fallen, but he was too weak to lift himself and move it. In the creek, a slender snag bobbled in the unhurried current with a constant swirling sound.

"He won't think to look here for me," Jesse thought. "He wouldn't never in God's world find me."

When morning came he walked to the house of his married sister, with whom he lived. Black lightwood smoke curled from the kitchen chimney, and he was about to go in when a fearful thought came: *Suppose he's setting in there right now, a-waiting on me?* He stopped. Then cautiously he eased into the woods and went around and came out back of the house. Stooping low, he went to the kitchen window and raised his head. His sister was at the stove, pouring boiling water from the black kettle over the dishes.

"Florella!" he said softly.

She turned her round face toward him. "Jesse," she said, "what's ailing you? Where you been?"

"Is anybody been here?" he whispered.

"Who?"

"Anybody come looking for me?"

"No, they ain't. What's ailing you? Come on in here."

He went around to the back steps and went in. He hung the muddy guitar on a wall nail.

"Who you think come looking for you?" Florella asked.

"A fellow said he might come by to see me about that milk cow."

"Well, he never come. Where you been at, all night?" Her face was almost handsome, except for the looseness of her red mouth. Suddenly she looked at him more closely. "Jesse, where in heaven's name you been at?"

"Out coon hunting with some fellows."

She grinned wisely. "Looks more like you been out with Cousin Silas and Bud Dorson."

He went into his room and shut the door. Deep in his wooden locker he unearthed a small, ugly derringer. Its handle curved under, toward the muzzle of the short barrel. He had bought it over a year ago, when he went with the posse to hunt for Tom Keefer. He cocked the gun, then let the hammer gently back into place. He did this several times, and slipped the gun into his overall pocket. "Now, Mr. Thursday," he said, "let's see you start something!"

But the feel of the gun against his leg made him uneasy, as it always did, and he put it back into the trunk.

Next morning, Thursday was waiting for Ben. "Well," he said, "I see you come back."

"I had made up my mind to come back sometime another, fore I left," Ben said.

"Well, you took your time about it."

"You cain't just go hopping into that swamp and right back the same day."

Suddenly Thursday's big, red-haired hand grasped the front of Ben's overalls. "I told you to be back in two days. You gitting to be just too damn biggety, but I'm still the man that can slim you down, you hear me?"

"I might a been panther-bit, for all you know," Ben protested.

"No, you wasn't panther-bit! You was just butt-headed. Just goan show me!"

"You wouldn't care noway. It wouldn't matter none what happened to me," Ben said.

"How come you think I told you to be right back?" Thursday demanded.

"To show me you was the boss, that's how come!"

Thursday shook him savagely. "I still aim to show you, too!"

Hannah stood in the door watching, her hand tight-shut against her mouth. Out in the yard, one of the hounds barked.

Ben wrested free, and jumped behind the bed, his face white, watching Thursday.

"You come here," Thursday said, heavily.

"Listen, I ain't coming there. I ain't goan fight my own daddy."

"I know you ain't. You just goan stand and take it."

"No I ain't, and that's why I ain't coming." Without taking his eyes off his father, he said, "Step here a minute, Miss Hannah."

She came to him swiftly. "What you want, Ben?"

"See what you see on the back of my head."

She parted his thick black hair, and gasped, "You've hurt yourself, Ben!"

"That's how come I was two weeks getting back." He looked at Thursday bitterly. "Not that he gives a damn."

Thursday came around the bed. Ben stood tense. Thursday said, "Let's see, son." He looked at the healing cut on Ben's head. "You could a told me, and saved all this ruckus. How did you git a lick like that, right by yourself out in the swamp?" Thursday asked.

"That ain't nobody's business but mine."

Thursday moved back a little and looked at him for a moment. "I don't aim to keep a-wrangling with you, Ben. You just mind from now on, and we won't have no trouble."

"Listen, Papa. I got my own bread to earn. That means I'm my own man. I cain't do everything you say do."

"Well, you just stay out of that swamp, and I won't ask much more outn you. I don't want to see you hurt. Many a man's gone into Okefenokee and never come out. You see what happened to you."

"I might as well tell you now then. They's more coon and otter in the swamp than I ever seen. I'm goan go to trapping the swamp, come wintertime, and maybe go deerskin hunting some in between.

If we got to have more argumint, we might as well git it over with right now."

Thursday's massive face darkened beneath his clay-red beard. "Ben, you ain't going into that Okefenokee no more, not and live under this roof with me." He turned and walked out. They heard his footsteps down the back steps, presently heard the jingle of plow chains as he hitched the mule.

"I reckon he'll git done with the bottom field this morning," Hannah said, hesitantly. "He's been worrying hisself about you, Ben."

"He won't have to, no more," Ben answered, and went to his room. Into his faded duffel bag he stuffed his overalls, his old dog-bed sweater, and his good shoes. He was collecting his odds and ends when Hannah followed him into the room.

"Ben, please don't do thataway. He'll git over it. Don't leave, Ben."

"You ought to see I got it to do," Ben said, looking for his hair comb.

"I cain't stand for you to go, Ben," she pleaded. "Ben, I love you like you was my own boy. Don't go leave me."

"You ain't old enough to have no grown boy," he answered, grinning fleetingly.

"Won't nobody take care of you like I do."

"Martin's got a empty nigger house on his place I imagine I can git. I'll be taking my own care of myself, and you know I can do a good job of that."

She sighed and began helping him. There wasn't really much to do, once he got his few clothes together. "Better take them bed sheets along, I reckon."

"I ain't taking nothing of hisn. This here blanket's mine, and I expect hit'll have to do me."

He went outside and got his rusty traps. Trouble's tail lifted excitedly when he saw the gun. He raised his wide nose and rumbled at Ben.

"Shut that big mouth and come on," Ben said.

Hannah walked to the gate with them. "Don't keep being mad at him, Ben. I guess he cain't see his boy is growed up. They's a lot of things Thursday don't see."

"I ain't mad at him."

"Will you be coming to see me along?"

"If going called for not seeing you no more, Miss Hannah," Ben said, "I'd stay and put up with anything."

He kissed her and started down the road, with Trouble running ahead and busily scenting the wire grass along the edge of the field. Over the rise, he saw his father, far down the bottom, plowing. At the end of the furrow, the distant man stopped and studied the ground, and Ben knew he was looking for fox tracks; but he'd see none on that dry ground today. Thursday lifted the plow around, then stopped, seeing Ben. Ben shifted the bag to his other shoulder and kept walking.

Thursday stood straight, looking at him; then he flicked the reins. The mule started forward again.

After he had installed himself in the little house on the farm of Martin, the storekeeper, Ben headed straight for the home of Tulle McKenzie. Tulle was a quiet, patient man; although he was only a little older than Thursday his hair — what there was of it — was muddy gray and wrinkles like quail tracks crisscrossed his face. Lately he had become a little deaf, and the folks who knew his wife said this was a blessing.

"Howdy, Ben," Tulle said.

"Howdy, Mr. Tulle. Hit's fixing to put in to raining, ain't it?"

"Yes, sir, fixing to go at it," Tulle said, looking at the gray-bottomed clouds, the gusty wind that shook the heavy leaves of the pear tree in the yard. "Hear tell you've been out into the swamp."

"That's right," Ben said, looking around.

"Eh?"

"I said that's right," Ben shouted. "Been in her two weeks, just messing around."

"Mabel's out in the lot feeding the chickens," Tulle said. "Guess that's who you come to see."

"That's who I come to see, all right," Ben said, and went down the big hall that divided the house. Mrs. McKenzie stepped out of the kitchen to speak to him, her angular face red from the heat of the stove.

"You been gone a long time, Ben," she said, showing her teeth in a cold smile. "Better watch your step, my lad. They's been other visitors around in your absence."

"Reckon I'll have to give a little somebody a talking to," he said lightly.

She showed her teeth again. "A young lady cain't be expected to save all her time for somebody that stays gone off so much."

Ben descended the steps. He heard Mabel's voice, "*Chick-oo, chick-oo, chick-oo . . .*" Around her the chickens and guineas gathered excitedly, and two fat white ducks kept pushing and shoving. Beyond the barn was the cow lot, and beyond it the flat fields of Tulle's big farm. Eight turkeys came running to join the feeding fowl, the leader an old bronze gobbler with a foot-long beard. Mabel's back was toward Ben. He leaned against the board fence and watched her.

"Goan git wet if you don't hurry it up," he said presently.

She turned and saw him, and dropped the feed pan. The fowl scrambled wildly over the spilled cracked corn. Ben climbed the fence to meet her, and to get her kiss. She clutched him tightly, then dropped her head against his chest.

"Don't guess that's no way for a nice girl to behave," she said.

"That's the way I want my girl to behave when I come to see her," Ben said, proudly, feeling a quick warmth.

"Ben, I thought you wasn't never coming back. I was afeerd you was kilt," she said. "Look, hit's raining a'ready!"

They started toward the gate, but then the water came flooding down, and they ran to the barn. Ben fumbled at the latch in the blinding rain, finally got it loose, and they climbed into the harness room and shut the door. Outside, rivulets flowed about the barnyard, but the fowl stayed on, feeding.

"Hit's dark in here, ain't it?" Ben said.

"I'm purely soaked!" Mabel moaned.

The rain thundered on the shingle roof overhead, and they could hear it running off the eaves in a cascade. Gradually their eyes made use of the light that filtered through the barn cracks. Old harness hung on rusty nails. There was a chair with a broken rocker, a grindstone, a pile of hay, the smell of grain and cattle and leather.

Mabel's thin work dress clung to her damply, and Ben thought that if she could see how she looked she wouldn't complain about being wet. He pulled her to him. "Good old rain," he murmured.

"I'm as wet as a goat," she kept saying.

"Let's sit down in that hay, long as we got to wait here."

"No, it'd stick to me."

Ben kissed her. "It's shore a satisfaction to find out somebody missed me while I was gone," he said.

"How come you stayed so long, Ben? Didn't you know I'd be worried near-bout to death?"

"I come out quick as I could."

She drew away from him. "No, you never. You could a come out a heap quicker. You don't have no thought of me at all, Ben."

"Yes, I do."

"No, you don't. But it don't matter. I have other visitors who are more concerned about my feelings."

"If I catch 'em around here, they goan be concerned about they own feelings," Ben said, pulling her to him again. "I come out that swamp quick as I could git out, and I ain't in no argufying mood, so you might as well hug up here and be quiet."

The rain continued its dull pounding, and the damp air became cold. They sank into the hay, their bodies close and warm against the wet chill.

Ben said, "I run off from home today."

He told her about it. And in her he found the sympathy he had wanted. An affection for her suddenly almost overwhelmed him. They talked on, companionably, and Ben thought that it was almost like the way a man and wife would talk.

"They's something I want to tell you," Ben said, finally. "I ain't going to be nobody's tramp in time to come. I'm goan be a first-class trapper. I aim to fill up that nigger house with hides, come wintertime. They won't be nobody around here I'll have to say 'sir' to."

"You're just talking big again, Ben."

"No I ain't. And I'm goan buy me a saddle horse, and a fine hound bitch to raise me some little Troubles." He shivered with expectancy. "And not long afterwards maybe I'll be around here with a proposition to make you."

She laid her head on his shoulder, and murmured, "What kind of proposition?"

"You'll find out. I'm going into Okefenokee, a-trapping. You never seen the like of hide animals."

She stiffened. "Ben, you'll lost yourself in that swamp, and I won't never see you again."

"No, I won't," he said, his blood rushing in the excitement of thinking about it. "I got me a partner that knows Okefenokee."

"Who?"

"I cain't tell you that."

"How come?"

"Well, because he's hiding. Now don't ask me no more."

She was silent a moment. "It's that nigger that killed his wife!"

"No it ain't. It ain't no nigger."

"Yes, it is. Ain't nobody else from around here run off."

"I tell you what let's do. Let's figure out who it is been coming to see my girl," Ben suggested.

"Just a friend."

"Well, you tell just-a-friend he's trespassing without my permission."

"A girl can't just settle down to one, Ben. Especially one that don't show up except when the notion strikes him."

"I better not catch nobody around here, that's all," Ben said mildly. He raised up, listening to the diminishing rain. The water dripped steadily from the eaves and ponded up all around the barn.

"My friend asked me to meet him at the sing Sunday."

"I thought you was goan meet me."

"Well, I didn't exactly know," Mabel said.

"Well, you know now."

She kissed him on his cheek, then drew back quickly before he could take hold of her. A rat started across the floor, saw them, and ran back under a crokersack of shelled corn. Mabel stared at the sack, and said:

"I cain't figure out who it could be in the swamp."

"Well, quit trying. And don't you never tell nobody. They might come in there looking for that nigger, and find this other fellow, and then my trapping would be over."

"You know I wouldn't tell nobody. I got a reason for wanting you to make good, ain't I?"

"I said as much."

"I'll be scared all the time you're in that swamp," she complained. "Hit ain't right for you to keep me scared that way, Ben."

"Nothing to be a-scared for."

"I'll be, though. Hit ain't right for you to treat me that way."

Ben grinned. "Let's git out afore you talk me outn it. The rain's about quit."

Outside, the earth had a clean, fresh-washed look. The wet chickens were still scratching around in the damp loam for corn.

"Guess you might as well pick out one them hens for me to fix for our dinner, Sunday," Mabel said.

"I want a full-grown 'un," Ben said, appraisingly. A fat dominicker hen caught his eye. In a moment the hen was flopping about in the water, its red, headless neck spurting. When the chicken lay quiet, he picked it up and slung the water and blood off, and handed it to the girl.

"I guess one will be enough," he said.

"Hit'll have to be," she said.

* * *

All-day sing,
Dinner on the ground,
Whisky in the bush
And women all around.

It was the finest sing that had ever been held, from the looks of the buggies and wagons tied up in the woods all around the churchyard, and the people in their go-to-meeting clothes, and the dinner the womenfolks set. The leader raised his fork, and the pinewoods rang. There were quartets and solos and then all-togethers.

Mabel was all prettied up, and flushed with excitement. She went about busily, cleaning up, and talking to the grown ladies.

"Why don't you just be still some, here with me?" Ben complained.

"I'll be back," Mabel said. "Yon's Mrs. McArthur, that used to live across the creek from us. I'll be right back."

Ben wandered about moodily, threading through the people. He looked up suddenly to see, right in front of him, his father and Miss Hannah.

"Howdy," Ben said.

"Howdy, Ben," Hannah said. "You gitting along all right?"

Thursday said, "I see you left my bed and board."

"I figured you'd notice it sometime another," Ben answered.

"I ain't goan beg you to come back."

"I know you ain't."

Hannah said, "Y'all don't start that, now. We're here to enjoy ourselves. Ain't the singing fine, though?"

"Pretty good singing," Ben admitted. "I liked that one Jesse Wick sung, but I believe he's better when he's just walking down the road by hisself."

Hannah colored, but Ben didn't notice it. "He's got a nice singing voice," she said faintly.

Silas Dorson took Ben's arm, and spread his harelip in a smile of greeting to them. Bud Dorson stood near by, hardly as tall as Hannah.

"How y'all gitting along?" Silas asked.

"Just tol'able," Thursday said. "How y'all gitting along?"

"Just tol'able," Silas answered. "If Miss Hannah will excuse y'all a minute, we got a little something to talk to you about."

Thursday and Ben followed the Dorson brothers through the maze of wagons and buggies

74

and unhitched mules and horses, until they came to the Dorsons' buckboard, where Jesse Wick waited with a jug of red whisky.

"Hello, Thursday," Jesse said with hesitant affability.

Thursday nodded to him unsmilingly. Bud Dorson pointed to the jug. "Well, you see we never brung you off for nothing."

Jesse held the jug toward Thursday. "Take yourself a pull at this, Thursday."

Thursday looked at Silas. "This what you wanted with me?"

"We knowed you couldn't sing on no dusty throat."

"I do my drinking somewheres besides in a churchyard," Thursday said. "Ben he can do like he wants. He's his own man now." He turned and left them.

"Well, you don't hurt my feelings none!" Silas called after him angrily.

"Give the jug to Ben. He ain't no human God A'mighty like his pa," Bud said. "What you trembling about, Cousin Jesse? Give Ben Ragan a drink of that panther water."

"Much obliged," Ben said, "but I just et."

"You got to wash it down then."

Ben took the jug and drank, and handed it back. When the jug had passed around, Silas licked his tongue into his split lip and said:

"They tell me you've done been into Okefenokee."

"Just went to git my hound," Ben said.

"You said you was goan take us," Bud said, leaning toward him accusingly.

"No, I never. Anyway, I never went hunting or nothing. Just looking for that damn hound."

"What's she like in there, Ben? Hit ain't hard to find your way around, I don't reckon, like they say."

"You'll get lost before you can turn on your heels," he said, discouragingly. "How come you think it took me two weeks to git out, after finding my dog the very first day?"

"My God, is that right?"

"You see any egrets, er coons, er anything much?" Silas asked.

"Naw, just mostly gators and cottonmouths."

"He's lying hard as he can go!" Bud accused.

"No he ain't, Bud," Silas said. "Ben wouldn't lie to us, not after drinking our whisky, and what else we goan do for him."

"Tell him," Bud suggested, grinning.

"Ben, we found us another rookery. She's

7 6

down the Suwannee a good piece. Before long she'll be ripe, and when me and Bud go, we're goan take you with us. What do you think of that?"

A girl in a white dress was laboring toward one of the buggies with a big basket of empty dishes.

"That's fine," Ben said, watching the girl.

"We wouldn't do it for nobody else. I expect we'll be hunting some more together along. Maybe even in that swamp."

"That's fine," Ben repeated absently. "Much oblige for the set-up." He walked around the buckboard and started toward the black-haired girl.

"We'll let you know!" Bud called.

The girl changed the basket from one side to the other as Ben reached her. Her eyebrows were smooth black crayon marks, and when Ben spoke to her, one of them rose a bit, curiously, as if of its own accord.

"That looks mighty heavy for you to tote," Ben said.

"I can tote it, though, much oblige just the same."

"I'd just as soon tote it for you," Ben said. "I ain't got nothing else to do."

"I brung it out, and it with dinner in it then.

Much oblige just the same." She did not look at him, but kept walking. Ben walked beside her. "If you don't let me tote it, I won't have no excuse to talk to you, and I'll have to go back."

She handed the basket to him. Her teeth were white but not quite straight. "I guess you ain't goan be satisfied until I let you," she said, flexing her cramped arms. "Papa was goan fetch it out, but he's in that next quartet."

"Who's your papa?"

"Felt Gordon."

"I don't believe I made his acquaintance. Y'all must be from off somewheres."

"We just moved here from Alabama." She indicated a bright new buggy. "Thatn's it."

He set the basket down. "Hit's a right pretty buggy."

She climbed up into the seat and sat down, and touched her mouth with her handkerchief. She had perfume on herself. Ben could smell it.

"Much oblige for helping me," she said. "I'm goan set here a spell and rest. You go on back."

Ben leaned against the empty shafts, and said, "I'm sort of petered out myself. Guess I'll rest a spell too."

"You'll miss some of the singing."

"I'll have a sufficiency of singing before the sun goes down, I imagine," he said. "You didn't tell me your name, that I remember."

She held her head sideways, listening to the distance-muffled "There Is a Fountain." Her hair — not black, he saw now, but deep brown — curled around her ear. Her eyes, he had noticed, were brown too, with yellow flecks; she was big and high-breasted, like Miss Hannah, only slimmer.

"You still ain't told me," Ben insisted.

She looked down at him, and that right eyebrow lifted again, absently. "Do strangers just start talking to each other around here?"

"Shore they do. It ain't Christianlike to keep being strangers."

"My name's Julie."

"Pleased to make your acquaintance. They call me Ben Ragan. I — look, what makes your eyebrow do that way?"

"What way?"

"Sort of go up all by itself, like it don't know it's attached onto you?"

"Hit just don't know no better, I guess."

"Nothing ain't wrong with it?"

"Nope."

"Hit's shore a curiosity," Ben said. "Well, I

reckon I better be a-rambling on back, er somebody'll be looking for me."

"Much oblige for helping me," she said.

"Look, in a day or two I'm goan be heading back into Okefenokee Swamp, but when I git out I might come set with you sometime another, if I ain't got nothing else to do."

"If you're a mind to," she said without enthusiasm.

Now as he poled toward the swamp, with Trouble tied in the front of the boat, the new girl was on his mind. It was the first time any girl had ever managed to take his thoughts away from Mabel McKenzie. "Expect I better not do no setting with her," he thought uneasily.

On the riverbank a coon stopped peeling a frog to stare at him. Trouble yelped, then leaped wildly overside, only to be snatched short by the rawhide leash. The coon vanished into the thicket, carrying the frog in his mouth. Trouble churned the water, swimming, trying to tow the boat. Kneeling, Ben moved to the bow, and dragged the dripping, eager dog back into the boat.

"Durn your bullheaded soul," Ben exclaimed, "I'm goan learn you some manners if I have to wear out a hickory on you!"

But after a while his anger at Trouble passed, as it always did, and he thought proudly, "Danged if he wouldn't a towed us right on to shore after that coon, and fer all I know, drug me right on through that thicket, boat and all!"

The swamp had never seemed more wonderful. Green it was, from the maiden cane to the cypress tops, so green it almost hurt your eyes. The gators were lazy, hardly bothering to slide off their sunning logs, or to sink in front of the boat. This day they seemed to be everywhere. It had been said that you could walk across Okefenokee on gator backs, but Ben figured he wouldn't want to try it. Herons and bitterns and poor joes rose at every turn, some of them squawking, spilling their frightened droppings into the black water. Once a water turkey thrust its snaky head above the surface, then disappeared beneath the water rather than use its wings, because it didn't fly well with wet feathers. Ben wished he could sing like Jesse Wick; he'd make the swamp echo today.

Tom Keefer waited for him at the head of the lake.

"You see I never brought no sheriffs," Ben said.

"I knowed you wouldn't," Keefer said. "You ought not to be carrying that dog around in a boat with you. I've heard tell a gator will turn over a boat to get to a dog. You ought to leave him here with me."

"I ain't leaving him nowhere," Ben said. "Anyway, where would I tell folks he was at, when I went out the swamp?"

As they poled toward the camp, Ben's boat following in the other one's rippling wake, Ben told him about Trouble and the coon.

"Maybe that coon was the daddy of the one I got at camp," Keefer said over his shoulder. "Caught a young 'un in a blueberry bush right after you left. He bit me some at first, but now he's tame as a house cat. Only he steals everything he can git his hands on."

"Well, you better keep him out of this dog's sight, if you think much of him."

Keefer stood on one bony leg, and rubbed a mosquito bite on it with the other, the smooth rhythm of his poling unbroken. "We'll teach Trouble better," he grunted.

Tom Keefer's half-grown coon scuttled toward them when they reached camp. Trouble immediately sounded off and hit the end of the leash, and there threshed about, half-choked. The coon watched the display curiously, its back arched, then ran into Keefer's hand and climbed to his shoulder.

"He stole my knife yesterday," Tom Keefer said, "and I like to never found it. The way I done, I put that bottle of matches you give me out where he could git it, and let him steal it too, and watched right where he went — into that hollow stump yonder. And that's where my knife were."

Keefer put the coon upon the branches of an oak sapling, and tied him there until they should teach Trouble his lesson, then he went to the shelter and came out with a strip of burnished leather. He knelt beside Trouble affectionately, and said, "I got you a present, mister."

"Now won't he be something, with a fancy gator-hide dog collar?" Ben said.

"I didn't have nothing much else to do," Keefer said, fastening the collar on with its rawhide laces.

"I believe you'd steal my dog if I was to give you half a chance," Ben said.

"I'd like to, and that's the God's truth, but I guess my stealing days are over."

After they had cooked and eaten, they decided to teach Trouble to leave the coon alone. They put the leash on Trouble. Then they turned him loose. Trouble went balling the jack for the coon, and Ben shouted, "Whoa!" Trouble didn't stop, and hit the end of the cord and was jerked over on his tail. They brought him back and turned him loose again, and again he didn't stop at the command. And again. For an hour they worked with him, and still he went for the now-sleeping coon. "Hit's a wonder his neck ain't broke," Ben said wearily.

The afternoon waned, and the wood ducks passed overhead in winnowing flight on their way to roost. In the distance a wildcat whined drowsily, getting ready for the night's hunting. Trouble still was after the coon, though he had bitten his tongue bloody, and he was gray with dirt.

Keefer built a fire, and was preparing to cook the pork Ben had brought, when Ben shouted, "He done it! Stopped when I told him!"

Trouble stood at the end of the cord, looking back at Ben. Ben drew the hound back and released him. Trouble started out, hard as ever, but when Ben yelled, he stopped, and stood still, glaring at the coon.

"Well, I guess he finally learnt, but he took God's own sweet time about it."

"Trouble ain't nobody's fool," Ben said.

In the days that followed, the coon became fond of Trouble, and would approach the sleeping dog to paw playfully at his face. Trouble tolerated this, but he never learned to like it. He would growl for a moment and, if the coon persisted, get up and move away. And whenever Ben said stop, from then on, Trouble stopped.

Keefer said, "Won't be much doing until wintertime. We could git some buckskins, only I don't expect they're worth a hell of a heap."

"We got it to do, anyhow. We'll need a big lot of new traps, if we hope to make any money on hides."

Keefer squatted on his knobby legs, staring thoughtfully into the fire. "I'll be glad when the money starts coming in."

"There ain't a great many stores in Okefenokee to spend it at," Ben said, curiously.

"I had a long time to set and think about it," Keefer answered. "I could git out of here, easy enough. But I couldn't go far before somebody seen me, somewhere around here, and maybe turnt me up. But if I had the money fer it, I could sneak into Waycross er somewhere and catch me a train right on down into Florida. Then wouldn't nobody never catch me."

"What you goan do in Florida?"

Keefer stared out toward the water. Finally he said, "I'd find me a somebody and git married, and raise me a fine family, and start me a new life all over. I been studying it all out a long time." He stood up and kicked a coal back into the fire with a bare foot. "Maybe hit won't never happen, but hit's all I think about."

PART III

Tom Keefer's knife traced an outline on the piece of buckskin, and he lifted out a piece of leather that somewhat resembled a lizard. To it he fastened five fishhooks, and the dabbler was finished. He tied the lure onto a pole, on a ten-inch string. Then he sat in front of the boat, and while Ben slowly and silently paddled him, Tom made the dabbler dance enticingly on the surface of the water ahead of the boat, running in and out of the marsh bushes. Presently the water boiled behind the dabbler. Keefer grunted, "Missed." In a few minutes again the water erupted beneath the lure, and it disappeared. Keefer quickly drew the pole in, hand over hand, and thrust his fingers into the wide-flaring gills of a four-pound bass.

"Come in out of the wet, old trout," Tom Keefer said, "afore you catch cold."

By the time Ben had shoved the boat back to camp, Keefer had the bass scaled and gutted and ready for the pan. While they waited for the fire to lower, Keefer inspected the hooks on his new dabbler.

"Believe this 'un's goan be a better fish-catcher than that 'un the mudfish tore up for me," he said.

Ben mealed the fish. "I expect you've got a bait of trout fish and deer meat in over a year of it."

Keefer said reminiscently, "I nearly lost my senses right at the first. But it weren't what I had to eat. The gators and snakes kept me scared, and at night they was noises fit to touch a man in the head. One night a bunch of wild hogs took after me, and I had to just cold outrun 'em." He poked at the fire. "I didn't know, neither, but what they might still be some Indians left in here somewhere. I ain't seen none, though, less you count bones. I dug into a mound, oncet, looking fer me some tools, and run up a skeleton seven foot tall."

"I never even seen no Indian, live er dead."

"I used to hunt with a half-breed oncet, before I got into all that trouble. That's how come I headed for Okefenokee. I figured if Indians made out in it, I could," Keefer said. "I tell you something I bet you never knowed. The Indians had them a Jesus."

"A Jesus?"

"Yes, sir. They said long time ago, the Great Spirit sent down a son of hisn, to live with the Indians, and learn them what was right and what wasn't."

"I wouldn't put much stock in what no Indian Jesus said."

"They had them a princess that was plumb beautiful. They toted her about on a stretcher-like, with gals fanning the yellow flies and skeeters offn her. After I had been in the swamp a spell, I use to make out that princess was my girl. Made out she slept with me and everything. I figured her to be light-colored, with gold ear-rings, and her hair soft, not stringy like regular Indian hair."

Ben thought about Julie Gordon, sitting up in the buggy. He even remembered how she smelled, and the way her eyebrow acted, and the little handkerchief she touched to her mouth. Then the rainy afternoon came back to him, and Mabel's damp warm body against his in the hay. He said, "I'd rather have me a white girl, that I didn't have to fan no skeeters offn."

"I don't know. Living out here, and messing around in they mounds, I got to where I'm nearly-bout Indian myself. You watch me now, and I'll show you how come you never heerd of no Indian hollering er cutting up when he was hurt."

Keefer brushed his hands off carefully, and squatted beside the fire. He stirred the embers until he found a glowing coal about the size of a walnut. With his left hand he calmly picked the coal up and placed it in the open palm of his right hand.

"You goan hurt yourself, showing off that-away," Ben said.

Keefer said nothing, just held the hot coal steadily. Ben smelled burned flesh. Tom Keefer's eyes grew vacant, as if his mind were elsewhere. He watched the coal until it cooled and turned black; then he removed it, and placidly replaced it with another glowing coal from the fire. When this one had cooled, he turned his hand over and let it fall.

Ben looked at the blackened palm. "Now your hand ain't goan be fit fer nothing in a week."

"Hit'll be nearly-bout well tomorrow," Tom Keefer said. "I reckon we can git the fish started, now."

"Didn't it hurt?"

Keefer shook his head. "I made up my mind not to let it."

"I don't see no sense in nothing like that," Ben said, setting the pan on the fire.

A bull gator flattened his head above the water and bellowed a greeting to the new morning. Farther down the swamp, another answered, and another, and then the echoes threw the sounds back.

"Them's my roosters a-crowing," Keefer explained, as they got ready to go deer hunting.

"Ain't you goan take old Trouble along?"

"Not this time. Won't need that gun, neither."

"You aim to trap them deer, er lasso 'em, er what?"

"With a little luck, I'll show you how to kill one with a stick."

They shoved off, with Trouble tied up, mournfully watching them. The sunrise was a crimson smear behind the green cypress forests; the thrushes on the islands made their raspy noises, and once an ivory-billed woodpecker vaulted overhead with his imperial, raucous cry, his beak glinting in the early light. After a while the swamp opened up and spread before them a wide, bonnet-covered, shallow-water prairie. A great raft of ducks fed peacefully. The wading birds stood motionless on stilts, solemnly staring into the water. In the center of the prairie, an eagle guarded his great nest of sticks in a lone, moss-hung cypress. Near the tree, a buck and a doe fed peacefully, thrusting their heads into the dark water for tender water-grass shoots.

Keefer passed Ben a five-foot hickory stick, hardly as thick as a man's wrist. "Now just set close and be fixed," he said, and suddenly sent the boat out into the prairie.

In spite of the boat's speed, there was almost no sound except the whisper of the bonnets against it, and it was halfway to the deer before the buck looked up with a snort of surprise. Even then they stared curiously a moment before they moved. At once Ben saw that the thing was possible. In the mucky bottom, the deer ran with leaden feet, in grotesque, painful jumps. And now the boat skimmed over the water. When the deer were within thirty feet of land, the boat caught them. The doe was behind. She swerved frantically, almost falling. But the boat skillfully turned with her.

"Give him a good lick!" Keefer shouted.

Ben swung the hickory, and it thudded against the doe's skull. She fell then, dropping to her haunches, and he struck again; this time she rolled over, roiling the water with spasmodic kicking. Ben waited a moment, then pulled her up close by an ear, and ran his knife blade through her throat.

"D'ruther had the buck, but they horns gits in the way sometime," Tom Keefer panted.

They camped on a palmetto island and dressed the deer, and hung her to drain. Meantime they walked out across the flat island. Around a little pond Ben found plentiful coon sign; overhead, an enormous flight of wild pigeons passed.

The sun was high now, and a warm wind put the palmetto fronds to rattling metallically. When Ben got thirsty, Tom dug a hole in the earth, and presently in it welled clean water, cleaner than they could have got from the pond.

Keefer hissed, "Git down!"

Beyond the thick screen of bay bushes, two

hundred yards out on the palmetto flat, a buck deer stood motionless, looking toward them. He was not a big animal; only his head and withers showed above the palmettos.

"Now's when we ought to have my gun," Ben whispered.

Keefer watched a moment, until the deer lowered his head and began feeding again, and said:

"Don't need no gun. You stay right here and don't make no noise."

He crawled out into the palmettos, inch by inch. Ben watched him until only a bare brown foot showed; for a long time the foot stayed there, then it disappeared. Ben noticed that the breeze was against his face, away from the deer.

An hour passed.

Not a bush had stirred to indicate Keefer's progress. The deer had fed down toward the pond they had left, occasionally raising his head alertly but without alarm. Ben's eyes hurt from trying to keep the animal in sight. He watched a buzzard wheel in the clouds, a black spot against the bright sky. A few mosquitoes found him, and he had to lie down flat to brush them off, so the deer wouldn't notice the sudden motion. The mosquitoes never seemed to bite Tom Keefer, he recalled in annoyance.

He got back to his knees just in time to see the deer lunge and then disappear, and a terrified bleat drifted to him.

Ben ran toward the spot where the palmetto bushes shook. The sharp fronds cut at his breeches, and once, in his eagerness, he stumbled and dived headlong into the brush. He regained his feet and ran again.

When he got there, Keefer was lying almost under the deer, with his arms and legs locked about it. The fresh-scarred earth showed the animal's struggles.

"Don't git close to them hoofs," Keefer panted, "er he'll cut you to pieces."

The deer's feet thrashed; his small antlers passed close to Keefer's head. Ben reached for his knife.

"Wait just a spell," Keefer said. "Now, look out!"

Keefer quickly disengaged himself from the animal and rolled free. At once the deer was on his feet, then in one great leap he cleared the brush and fled, bouncing across the palmettos with flashing white flag erect.

"How come you turnt him a-loose?" Ben demanded in amazement.

Keefer brushed himself off in silence. Finally he said, "Let's be gitting on to the boat."

Ben angrily seized his wrist. "That was a dollar and a half worth of buckskin you had a-holt of. How come you didn't let me stick him?"

Keefer said, "I don't know. Sometimes I git thataway. When I don't need the meat, just seems like it's hard to do. Every time I grab one like that, and hold him tight up to me, and feel the life pounding and fighting in him, I just ain't got the heart."

Ben stared disgustedly. "I see you goan be one ideal trapping partner."

"No, it ain't that way with coons and cats and otters and meat-eating critters. They kill what they eat, and they ain't got no right to ask not to be killed themselves. But deers don't kill nothing. Just eat grass and leaves, and stuff like that."

Ben kept muttering as they turned back toward the prairie. "They say you stole many a hog, and butchered them. Hogs eat peanuts and corn."

"I can't rightly put it into words. A deer is just different, when you got him live in your hands, and you got plenty of meat anyway," Keefer said. "I seen a sow eat her own litter of new-dropped pigs, oncet."

When they were still a distance from the prairie, they saw that the limb the doe hung from was shaking. A look passed between them, and they started running. Short of the clearing they slowed, and then, suddenly, they stopped.

A panther was trying to drag the deer from the tree. His hind feet were on the ground, and his teeth and front claws were deep into the carcass. He pulled at it, with a rumbling in his throat; and when it did not fall, he turned loose and went around to the other side, and attacked again.

"You git from there!" Ben shouted, outraged.

The panther dropped to a crouch and spat noiselessly at them, his tawny tail twitching. The deer swung slightly above him. Ears flattened against his head, the panther watched them, reluctant to leave the fresh meat.

Still furious, Ben picked up a lightwood knot and sent it whistling. The knot hit in front of the big cat, and bobbled toward him. He flicked it away with a lightninglike movement of his paw, then turned into the thicket behind him and disappeared into the shadows.

"If you'd a let me brought my gun, we'd a had

a panther hide to sell in place of that doeskin he tore up," Ben said bitterly. "Whyn't you run up and grab him like you done that buck?"

"I ain't crazy," Keefer said, examining the ruined hide.

That night the coon played on Keefer's shoulder, and Trouble, the hound, lay outside the rim of the firelight and watched the coon, like a cat watching a bird in a cage.

Ben lay stretched out peacefully.

"I don't see how come you want to leave a fine place like Okefenokee," he said.

"You'd see, if you was about ten years older, and not much hope of gitting out, and no wife to love you, and no kids to live after you," Keefer said, morosely.

"The swamp ain't dangerous that I can see, like they say."

"If you know it, hit ain't. But you could git lost and go plain crazy trying to git out. And some places hit's boggy, and a man would sink over his head," Keefer said. "They's a time when most of the Okefenokee critters will leave you be, and they's a time to leave *them* be. I wouldn't want to go a-washing in no gator hole at night, ner fool around them when they's a-rutting and the air smells of they musk. And it don't pay to git in the way of no bear that's cut off from the thicket. Panthers is bashful-like only hit ain't good sense to throw light'd knots at airn that's got him some fresh meat. Thatn today was half a mind not to run. They's a few critters, though, that don't aim to run from a body, and them you better not monk with. Like a timber rattler, and a cotton-mouth, and a pack of hongry wild hogs."

Ben said, curiously, "How come you stole all them hogs you did?"

"Just plain meanness, I reckon. Hit was sort of like hunting. I could've stole all the range hogs I wanted, but I got my enjoymint out of slipping right onto somebody's place, with yard dogs sleeping under the house, and coming out with a fat shote and not nobody catching me." He smiled in the semidarkness. "Don't guess they was never nobody could beat me at it."

"Looks like you wouldn't a picked on your own brother-in-law, though."

"I never stole nothing from Josiah Wick."

"Your own sister said so."

"I don't hold it against her," Keefer said. "There was just two of us children, me and her.

She was always scared-like, and I sort of protected her all the time. After she married Josiah, and he started abusing her, she used to come to me and cry near-bout all day long. I told him more'n oncet to treat her right, and he said I better stay out of his business. One day I caught him at it. I had my gun, and I just purely let him have it, right in the belly. But afterward, when I seen her taking on over him, I knowed I better git out o' there."

An insect whirred in a live-oak tree. Trouble tired of watching the coon, and dropped his ugly head on his paws in sleep.

"Don't he never hant you none?" Ben asked.

"I see him bumping around on the floor sometime, but that's about all."

Next day they took Trouble and the gun, and tried to pick up the panther's trail, thinking he might still be in the vicinity of the dead doe. Trouble leaped impatiently from the boat to shore, and ran here and there with his nose down. Down along the prairie shore, he let out a brief tentative bay. For a long time he was out of sight and silent, then suddenly a full-throated hunting cry rolled back to them.

"He's jumped a deer," Keefer said.

"That ain't his deer cry," Ben said excitedly. "That's his cat cry."

They started following the dog, trotting along the hard-earth pine island. For two hours they kept Trouble's trumpet blasts within hearing. Then the sound began to fade.

"That's a traveling panther cat," Ben muttered.

"He's got a something-another on his tail to make him travel," Keefer said.

Now the sound came back again, distantly, just as they reached the other side of the island. Keefer studied the ground for tracks, but found none.

"They've done left the island," he said. "Old Trouble made him take out acrost that marsh yonder. Wisht I could a seen it. They ain't nothing funnier than a panther trying not to git his feet wet."

They waited there for an hour. Again they heard the dog.

"Listen!" Ben said, catching a change of tone in Trouble's baying. "He's treed him!"

Keefer studied the terrain ahead of them. "Ain't but one thing to do, then, and that's git the boat and go around the other way."

For the rest of the morning and half the afternoon they shoved the boat, avoiding the boglands, and the sunless thickets, and the pin-down bushes whose branches grow back into the earth to form a snare for a man's foot. And always, when they lost direction, they could stop and listen, and presently Trouble's patient bell-like treed cry would set them right again.

They got as close as possible by boat, and struck out across the mucky trembling earth, with the bushes and trees forty feet away stirring as if on troubled waters. The earth itself would not support a man's weight. They stepped from old, half-petrified logs to cypress knees to gnarled root to matted brush. Finally they reached Trouble, who gave them a brief, impersonal wag of his tail and looked up into the white bay tree.

"Yon he is!" Keefer said.

Ben said, "I don't see him."

"Look in them leaves right yonder."

Now Ben made out the dark outline of the beast flattened into camouflage, like a swollen place on the bay limb. A feeling of foreboding shivered through him. Yesterday, the thing had been only a big cat trying to steal a deer. Now, half-hidden in the bay leaves, glaring malevolently at them, thinking its baleful thoughts, the silent thing was death itself.

"Hold that fool dog," Ben said, and raised the gun, with its heavy charge and nine lead buckshot.

He pulled the trigger. The panther leaped straight out into space, feet spread, like a gigantic flying squirrel, then fell to the ground with a sodden thump. At once he was up, and streaking away. He jumped halfway up the trunk of a gum tree, clinked a few quick feet, then leaped out backward and struck the muck. Again he ran, bouncing from log to tussock, his tail alive, every part of him vibrant. He started up another tree, and fell, and writhed in the muck in savage death contortions.

Trouble twisted in Keefer's grasp until he nearly choked; then he was free. When he got to the panther he locked his jaws into the tan throat.

"Come back here," Ben warned; "that cat could have his head shot off and still rip you open afore he died."

But the panther was dead, his head twisted under him, and bright blood bubbling in the buckshot holes. The tail tip stirred absently.

The afternoons were warm, now, and often Ben and Tom Keefer spent the first part of them drowsing under the big sycamore tree. The trunk of the tree was mottled, like the skin of a nigger Ben had once seen whose forehead and nose were black-tan and his mouth and chin white as his own. They had left Trouble untied until the day they woke and found that he had got restless and gone off. Ben went to look for him, blowing his horn, and when he saw him, the dog was swimming toward him across the lake, and behind him the head of an enormous gator, like a chunk of charred wood, followed. The gator could have caught him in one swift rush, for there are few things faster in the water, but he had not quite made up his mind. Ben threw up his gun and shot, and through the cloud of gun smoke saw the gator spring straight up, white belly flashing, even his great tail clearing the water, then fall back sideways, smearing spray. Surprised, Trouble turned and saw the gator for the first time, and like a fool turned back with a growl, and made a few belligerent circles at the bubbled spot where the injured reptile had disappeared. But the gator, though far from fatally hurt at that distance, was long gone.

"We got to be careful, er that dog'll shore git gator-et one o' these days," Tom Keefer said later. "We better not use him no more until winter, unless on a rawhide, slow-trail. In the cold of winter, the gators go in they caves, and even when they come out on warm days, they don't eat nothing much."

"If old Trouble was to git killed," Ben said slowly, "I'd be sorry I ever seen this swamp, no matter how rich I git offn it."

Keefer spread out one of the deerskins they had got that morning and began scraping it. "White folks always thought it was curious the way Indians buried a man's dog with him. Oncet I asked a preacher how come a dog didn't live another life, the way they say human folks do, and he said a dog didn't have no soul. You got a soul?"

"Shore I got a soul."

"Lemme see it."

"You cain't just pull no soul out to look at."

Keefer rolled the hide up. "They say a dog is dead when he dies, but human folks ain't. I don't see how come that should be. You take that coon yonder, trying to slip off with your cow horn. Ain't he got life in him, just like you? Ain't he got lights and guts and kidneys? If you got a soul, how come he ain't got one too? Didn't he git himself borned, and don't he breathe? How come his life's goan end when I git fed up on his devilmint, and kill him, if your life ain't goan end when you die? Look a-here at this yellow fly trying to git his sticker into my hide. Ain't he got life in him, just like me?"

Ben reached over and squashed the yellow fly. "Not now, he ain't."

"You ain't killed him. His life's just gone somewheres else. Just like Trouble's would've if that gator had a got him."

"You ain't making heaven out to be much of a place, if it's got yellow flies in it."

"Well, I ain't got no map of it, but I reckon the Lord knows how to run it. He give folks a life, and dogs a life, and flies a life, and I don't believe He said to the dog, 'Now thisn I'm a-giving you ain't good fer but a while, and when you git shed of it, you ain't got no comeback, you're just plain dead,' and then turnt round to the man and said, 'Thisn I'm a-giving you is my first-class job, you're such a fine fellow; and it won't never run out on you.'"

"The Bible don't say nothing about no yellow flies and dogs going to heaven."

"They's a heap the Bible don't say, and that's the trouble with it. You take Jesus now. He must a been a mighty fine man, but it wouldn't a been hardly no trouble fer him to tell a little more of what it's all about. If I'd been him, I'd a said, 'Now, folks, I know you're right curious about what heaven's like, and I'm goan tell you what's what, and you write it down.' And then folks'd know."

"Maybe he figured people didn't have sense enough to understand what he was talking about."

"A man smart as Jesus could a put it so they'd a got it. I've studied on it a right good deal, trying to think how I'd like fer heaven to be, and I just cain't make up my mind. I've thought, 'Maybe you just stay alive, and float around, like pipe smoke, forever.' But *forever*, that's a long time. That's from now on. Not just two or three hundred years, but thousands and thousands, with no end to it a-tall. God A'mighty, you just think about that! A hundred years er so might be all right, but *forever*, that's too damned long to be alive. I don't care how fine a place it is, I'd git tired of it in a thousand years.

"Then sometimes I think, 'Well, maybe you're cold dead when you die, and just don't never think er move again, just like them Indian bones —*forever*.' There you are again. That's from now on, too. You see? That's too long to be dead. I reckon God's a whole lot smarter than I am, but some time I git right curious to see just how He's got it worked out."

Ben looked at him suspiciously. "I don't think you believe in no God."

"Sometimes I think one way, and then another. When I look at some things that goes on in this world, I figure that if there's a God, He ain't much of one. And then I think, 'Well, maybe He knows what He's a-doing, and we just ain't got sense enough to see it.'

"And here's something else. If there ain't no God, then we just happened here, just borned of Nature, as some folks say. Well, Nature, now, she ain't got no sense of decency, cause she ain't got no sense. Yet animals' privates, they don't stick out, they're sort of hid, covered with hair, and tails covers they asses, and men and women got hair where it ain't fer no purpose but to kindly cover up, just as if Somebody thought it wouldn't be fitting fer living things to go around with everything showing. You'd have to turn that coon over and study him to see whether he was a he or a she. Don't that look like they's some thinking going on behind all this? Nature, she wouldn't a never thought of nothing like that, cause she cain't think. She wouldn't give a damn how critters went around, ner what showed."

Ben went and got his cow horn, which the coon had been dragging toward the brush by its rawhide neck cord.

"I guess you was aiming to learn to blow it," Ben said to the animal.

The coon sat motionless in disgust, then ambled across the camp to annoy the hound.

Ben traded the deerskins to Martin for ten new traps, and he turned the panther hide in for provisions and gunpowder for his next trip into the swamp, to be got whenever he was ready. On Martin's mare, Ben rode down and spent the rest of the afternoon with Mabel.

Finally she said, "I really would love to ask you to stay and eat with us, Ben, but I have a friend a-coming."

"That same friend?"

"Which one?" she asked.

"The one that's been a-coming."

"Miles Tonkin? Yes, he's the one."

"Well, I got somebody else I can go see, too," Ben said angrily.

"All right, get mad about it. You don't have

no thought of me, Ben. I never knowed you was coming."

"It don't matter. I got me a somebody else I can visit with."

"Who?"

"That's all right who."

"You wouldn't go off to see some other girl, Ben."

"Well, you just hitch up Mr. Tulle's saddle horse and follow me and find out fer yourself," Ben said.

"You ain't going nowhere but to that house you live in."

"Follow me and see," he said, opening the front gate.

As he galloped down the road, he thought, *I just hope I meet up with him on the way down there, that's all.* But he didn't, and he began to wonder if he really dared to go see Julie Gordon. He could remember the dress she had on, and the lukewarm look in her eye, but the picture of her face would not return.

On a pretext of wanting to sell Felt Gordon a saddle of venison, he found out from Martin where Julie lived, and finally he got up his nerve actually to go there. By the time he had gone back by his house and turned the horse east, dark had come. There was no moon, and Ben had to trust the horse to keep to the road.

Four miles later, a yard dog started barking, long before Ben saw the light of the house. Ben stopped the horse, and would have liked a minute to build up his courage, but the dog's barking was so insistent that he had to go on in.

"*Hello!*" he shouted, and the barking became frenzied. Presently the door opened, and Felt Gordon yelled the dog quiet.

"It's Ben Ragan, Mr. Gordon," Ben said, hesitantly.

"Git down and come in," Gordon said.

Ben hitched the mare and walked through the yard and mounted the steps, while the dog growled at him from beneath the porch.

"What did you say the name was?" Gordon said, only his head showing, and Ben knew one hand was on his gun.

"Ben Ragan. I live west o' here, on Martin's place. I — I brung y'all a piece of deer meat."

"Well, that's mighty nice," Gordon said suspiciously.

" 'Tain't nothing," Ben said. "Don't expect the meat's no good much. I — is Miss Julie to home?"

Gordon straightened. "Oh, I see." He opened the door wide. "Shore she's to home. Where'd you think she'd be at? Come in, son."

They were all seated around the lamp, Mrs. Gordon — a fine, leather-faced woman — and an old woman Ben figured was Felt Gordon's mother, and a girl child, and a boy about twenty or so. He was a Gordon, too, from the look of him, and he examined Ben critically and without friendliness. And Julie. Ben sat in the proffered cowhide chair with hardly a glance at her, and yet he thought, yes, that's the way she looked, all right.

"The young man brung us some deer meat," Felt Gordon said.

"That's mighty nice," Mrs. Gordon said.

Amos Gordon, the son, hitched forward and said, "Where'd you kill him at?"

"In the swamp."

"You ain't talking about Okefenokee?"

"Yes. I just come out."

Amos looked at him with a sudden respect. "Never knowed nobody went into that place."

"Don't nobody much, but me," Ben said casually. "We could use another good washing rain about now, couldn't we?"

"I'd shore like fer it to come one," Felt said, solemnly. "Don't care about seeing it myself, but I'd like for this little six-year-old gal here to see one. She slept through that other one."

They all laughed, the family somewhat dutifully, and Ben guessed that it was one of his stock jokes. Ben told them about the swamp, and how he had killed the panther. The hide was at Martin's if they happened to go to the store sometime soon — this to quiet the doubt in Felt Gordon's eyes. Amos and Felt kept asking him questions, and the womenfolks listened interestedly, all but Julie, who kept to her sewing, and Ben knew he was making a fine impression. This was confirmed when Julie, out of a clear sky, said:

"Mr. Ragan and I got acquainted at the sing."

"You like singing?" Felt asked.

"Yes, but I ain't much good at it. Wisht I was," Ben answered.

"I take to it. Amos there, he's got a nice bass — make the dishes rattle in the kitchen."

"They ain't hardly nothing prettier than good singing, less'n it's the noise of a pack of big-voiced hounds on a hot trail," Ben said.

"They tell me they's some fox hunters hereabouts," Felt said, leaning forward.

"We just come here from Alabama," Mrs. Gordon explained.

"Had some dogs, too, but they took sick and died," Amos said.

"If you're a mind to fox-hunt, I'd be proud if you'd join us. Martin lets on they's one tomorrow night."

"I'll shore come, and Amos too, if you say it's all right," Felt said immediately. "You got any hounds?"

"An old piece of one. Y'all will be welcome."

Gradually they drifted out, all but Julie, who kept to her sewing. Mrs. Gordon said she had to put the girl to bed, and the old woman went with her. Amos said he had to draw some water, and presently Felt just rose and said good-night and went out. Julie looked for another spool of thread.

"Don't reckon you hardly remembered me," Ben said, tentatively, not feeling nearly as bold as he had at the sing.

"I reckon I did," she said.

"Guess I didn't have no business coming, not knowing you no better."

"Hit's all right," she said.

"You said come, if I was a mind to."

She looked at him, and her eyebrow rose in that strange, unpredictable fashion. "What's the swamp like? I don't mean the deers and panthers and all. Is it any flowers in it?"

"I never took notice," Ben admitted. "Seem like they was some red things on vines, and yellow jessamine. Oh, yes, and they's some kind of stems sticking outn the water, brown, and then a band of white in the middle, and bright yellow on top. And blue water lilies, and white 'uns. And the hurrah bushes, they got pink flowers." He tried hard to think of some more flowers, and resolved to watch more carefully next time.

"Is it green in the swamp, or just muddy and graylike?"

"Hit's green, all right, plumb green. Maiden cane and cypress tops and palmettos and bushes. And even that black water is turnt green with the bonnets and cypress shadows."

She was entranced, and whenever he would mention something she would say, "What color was it?" He talked with less ease than when the family was present, but she drew him out. Once or twice he forgot and said "we," meaning Keefer and himself; but when she said, "I thought you was by yourself," he answered, "I meant me and that old crazy dog I take with me."

After about an hour, he told her he'd better be rambling, and when he actually did rise to go, another half-hour later, he said, "It might be I'll come back sometime another, if you ain't got no objection."

"I don't think of no objection," she told him.

Felt and Amos Gordon were there next night, as they'd said they'd be, and Ben made them acquainted around. Blind Fiskus leaned against a stump and fiddled *Run, Nigger, Run*, paying no heed to the talk, only the gurgle of the whisky jug or an experimental bugle from the distant hounds being able to distract him. There were eight hunters; occasionally one of them would say, *Listen a minute!* and the rambling talk would cease, and the man would finally shake his head and say, *Nope.* Thursday Ragan lay on his side, running a grass straw between his teeth, his beard black instead of red in the firelight. He had said "Howdy," and Ben had said "Howdy," and that had been the conversation between them.

Suddenly a hound's voice rose in the far bottom, with a profound echoing timbre as if the dog were baying into a well. The sound rolled again, fiercer.

They all had their backs to the fire, now, staring into the darkness beyond. Hardy Ragan said, "Your old butt-head has shore riz one, Ben."

Now the other hounds' voices joined in fiercely, but the racing Trouble was far ahead of them. The chase was between him and the fox, mainly.

"Boys, they just ain't no use a-talking," Martin said, after a while, his voice solemn. "We all got us good hounds and sorry hounds, but they ain't another dog on God's green earth like Ben Ragan's dog Trouble."

Hardy Ragan answered, "You've spoke the plain truth, Martin. That big chop mouth is got a note like Gabriel's own horn. And yonder poor fox had better git him into a tree and quick about it, cause that Trouble dog will ketch him if he stays on the ground. Only thing, Ben should a learnt him to be a strick fox dog, instead of running anything with feet."

Ben said, "That's the way I want him, only not so butt-headed."

Martin said, "I'll take him like he is. I'd swap

my whole pack fer him; yes, by God, and nearly-bout throw my store in to boot."

Ben was deeply moved. Polite praise of another man's hound was customary; but only the profoundest admiration would cause a man to come right out and class another's dog above his own.

Trouble's baying ceased abruptly.

"Lost 'im," Amos Gordon guessed.

"Lost 'im nothing. That's a dead fox," Thursday Ragan said, and Ben knew he spoke before he thought.

"If we hunted old Trouble much," Martin said, "we wouldn't hardly have no foxes left to chase."

It was on the way down to start the hounds off again that Thursday stepped into a stump hole. He grunted heavily, and when he tried to get to his feet, his right knee buckled, and he fell again. They supported him and examined the twisted knee by torchlight.

"Guess I'll have to do the rest of my fox-hunting tonight just sitting a-listening," Thursday panted.

"What you ought to do," Hardy Ragan said, "is to ride on home and git some biling cloths on it."

"Reckon that's right." He put his foot down, and gradually eased his weight onto it. "She's a mite better now."

"I'll git your horse," Ben offered.

"Hardy will git him," Thursday said shortly.

Thursday came in through the back field, riding high in the saddle to try to catch occasionally far-off music of the chase. But the sounds had faded, and he painfully dismounted and unsaddled the horse.

As he slowly made his way around to the front of the house — Hannah always let him in the front door — he stopped suddenly, hearing voices. His first thought was that marauders had come, and he limped quickly to the front porch.

"Hannah! Hannah! You all right?" he called.

Immediately a dark figure leaped from the porch and ran. "You stop, sir!" Thursday shouted angrily, hobbling out the front gate. But whoever it was kept running. Pounding footsteps rang down the road, and in the darkness Thursday followed, now managing to run too, unmindful of the slashing pain in his leg.

From the porch, Hannah stared fearfully into the darkness, listening to the sounds, and to Thursday's outraged shouting. A numb helplessness grasped her brain, holding it in cold hands. A faint breeze rustled the new leaves in the oak tree that overhung the house. From the bottom came the peeping of the little frogs.

Hannah moved, and her foot touched the guitar. For a moment she stared at the dim outline of it. There it lay, with its bright steel strings and fancy braided cord now invisible, its music stilled. Then, quickly, she picked it up and ran into the house.

Her thoughts ran wildly, *Where'll I hide it at?* Eventually the place occurred to her, and she hurried into Ben's room — the room that Thursday never went into now. The closet was unceiled, opening into the attic. Standing in a chair, reaching up, she pushed the guitar back into the darkness of the attic. She pulled the chair back into the room, and latched the closet door.

When she went uncertainly back to the porch, Thursday was coming in, panting, calling her.

"You all right, Hannah? Who was it? You all right?"

"Yes, I'm all right."

In the living room she lit a lamp with trembling fingers, hardly able to get the chimney properly seated in the sprockets.

"What was he up to?"

Hannah said nothing, just looked at him.

"What was he up to, Hannah?" Suddenly Thursday saw that she was fully dressed. For a long moment he stared at her, and finally a new thought seemed to come to him. "You know who he was, Hannah?"

"Yes."

He stood there staring at her, holding onto the corner of the table. He breathed heavily. "He wasn't trying to bust in, or steal nothing?"

"No."

"Oh, I kindly begin to see." Slowly he sank back into a chair, staring at her. Minutes passed. She had never seen him like that; a fury would have been more like him.

Hannah said, uncertainly, "What's the matter that you was limping? You hurt yourself?"

Thursday muttered, "And he's been a-coming, every night I was gone off."

"I got lonesome, Thursday."

"You told him when to come," he said slowly.

"No, I never. He just knowed when to."

Thursday kept watching her, and finally he breathed, "Miss Hannah, I just cain't hardly believe it."

"You was gone so much, and I got lonesome."

Thursday's red face hardened. "You'll have to tell me who it were."

"I cain't do that, Thursday."

"You got it to do."

"I ain't, though, Thursday. You'd go at him with your gun."

"Well, they ain't so many men in this country that I cain't figure it out fer myself," he said with cold anger. He struggled to his feet and limped back to the kitchen. Presently she heard him breaking splinters to build a fire in the stove. Then the well teakle squeaked as he drew a bucket of water. She went back to the kitchen.

"I wisht you'd tell me how you hurt yourself," she begged.

Thursday stolidly dipped water into a pot with the gourd.

"I can boil that water, and help you out," Hannah said.

He turned, and she had never seen a look like that on a man's face. "No, Miss Hannah," he said. "No, you cain't."

Hannah lay in bed, staring at the dim window. The silence of the night pressed heavily upon her, and her thoughts kept going around and around, and running into each other. After what seemed years, daylight began to break, and Thursday had not come to bed. She dressed. He was sitting by the cold stove, his fingers twisting in his red beard. On his bare, swollen knee lay a cloth that she guessed had been there, cold, for hours.

"I'll git breakfast started," she told him.

"I've et," he lied. He rolled down his trousers leg and hobbled out on the back porch.

By morning Jesse Wick was miles away. He didn't know where he was — he had turned north, he dimly remembered. His clothes were torn nearly off him, and his skin held smilax scratches and dried pencilings of blood. He kept to the woods, avoiding the roads and trails. Sometimes he walked, stumblingly; then a terror would strike him and he would run headlong, jumping logs and branches, falling, sobbing.

You better tell me who it were, Hannah, you know I ain't goan put up with such as this. Who were it I tell you. i cain't tell it on him, thursday. *Yes by God you will tell it on him. A-sneaking in here just time my back were turnt. I'll find him and you know what I'll do.* i never told him to come, thursday. he just come. i tried to run him off but he wouldn't go. this were the first time he come. i hollered for you, but you was off a-fox-hunting. *Well you tell me now. I'll fix him proper. Look a-here, Hannah, what's this guitar doing here? Well now I guess you don't need to tell me.*

Jesse Wick said, "Now I've done gone and lost my guitar. Don't know where I ever git me another one."

For two days he wandered, without eating. Finally he came upon a house in a clearing. Beyond was a field, and on the far side of it a man plowed a brace of oxen. Jesse lay in the brush and watched the house, patiently, like an animal. About the middle of the morning, a woman left the house and crossed the field to help her husband. The yard dog trotted behind her. Jesse crawled across the clearing and slipped into the back door. In the kitchen safe he found a piece of cold fish and some cornbread. He bolted all the food he could find, glancing out the back door to see that neither of the people would surprise him. His eye caught something hanging on the wall. A guitar. Quickly he took it down, held it lovingly.

From the next room came a strange sound.

Startled, Jesse peeped into the door of the bedroom. On the bed, a year-old baby, fresh wak-
ened, smiled at him and waved its arms. Terrified, Jesse ran through the room and out the
front door, clutching the guitar, and kept running until he was miles away. Hours later he sat
upon a stump, and tuned the guitar. Then he
sang softly, "*Somebody better come and git me,
my little wife's done gone and quit me. . . .*"

When Jesse Wick finally got home, several
days later, his sister screamed, and her husband came running, and finally they recognized
him.

"Where in the Lord's name you been, Jesse?"
Florella asked.

"Off to see a fellow."

"Where does he live at?"

"I disremember," Jesse answered, puzzled.

Florella's husband grinned. "He don't live in
no bottle, by any chancet."

Jesse brightened. "Might be."

"Where'd you git that guitar? That ain't
yourn," Florella asked.

Jesse stared at the guitar curiously, inspecting
it. "Guess I must've swapped with somebody,"
he said, finally. He ran his fingers across the

strings, and listened carefully. Then he said, "Plays good, don't it?"

They went in two boats, several miles down the Suwannee, Ben and Silas Dorson in one, Bud Dorson following in the other with the guns and plume bags. They had borrowed several guns, so there wouldn't be so much delay in reloading. Ben paddled indifferently. Martin had said he wouldn't like plume hunting; but if that were true, it would be the first kind of hunting he didn't like. He regretted coming, just the same, because if they had luck the Dorson brothers would expect to go with him to Okefenokee. He'd have to slip off without them, and when they found out about it they'd be mad, and, knowing them, he knew that might mean trouble.

Silas turned the boat up a stagnant slough, and after a while he turned it into the mudbank. "Here's where we start afoot, Ben. Now when we git there, you take this side, and me and Bud'll cross around. Don't let miss no birds, because the aigrettes on them long whites' backs is worth ninety cents."

They slogged through a mile of bogland up to their knees, and presently they reached the dead-water pond of the egret rookery. Through the brush Ben could see splotches of white — egrets. The Dorson brothers left him to circle the pond. When he decided they had had time to get around to the other side, he crept on to the edge of the water, carrying two smooth bores.

Some of the egrets now took alarm, flying off on strong wings. Knowing their wild ways, he thought, *Long gone now*. Some still stood near their nests, wings half spread, long necks alert. To his surprise, Ben saw that the others were now returning, gliding straight back in. One turned directly over him, legs outstretched, neck drawn back in a white "S." Ben followed the bird over the gun barrel, then fired. The egret crumpled into shapelessness and struck, and lay there like a bucket of snow dumped upon the water.

"That's the time, Ben!" Bud called. They were firing now, and more egrets fell. For a while, then, the birds left, but again they came back.

Ben heard a noise overhead, and he saw why the egret he killed had returned. Close to him, in a scrub cypress, was a nest, a haphazard affair of sticks, in which three young egrets stretched their necks hungrily toward the passing birds. Suddenly an empty sickness ran through him.

The young birds would starve; and there were hundreds of them in the other nests. The adult egrets had forgotten their shyness to return to protect their nests — and meet death.

Resolutely Ben fired the other gun into the air. Then he thrust his powderhorn into the water and held it under. He waded back to shore and left the guns.

The Dorson boys were too busy shooting to see him climb the tree and capture the young egrets. He descended, holding them all three by their legs. Cutting three holes in one of the plume bags, he thrust the birds inside, and by their long beaks pulled their heads through the holes. Then he tied up the sack and sat down to wait.

When it was over, and the Dorson boys were through floundering in the pond to pluck the silky aigrettes from the backs of the dead, floating birds, they came around to where he sat.

"What happened to you, anyway?" Silas demanded, wheezing through his harelip.

"I fell down and got my powder wet," Ben explained.

"Now if you ain't a fine plume-hunter!"

"How come you got to shoot these birds when they're a-nesting?" Ben asked.

Bud said, "Them plumes is mating feathers. And only when they got young 'uns is they fool enough to fly back and git shot."

"Well, I don't know as I exactly care about it," Ben said, coldly. "I ain't goan have none of the money."

They were too triumphant to take offense. Silas shrugged. "All the more for Bud and me."

Next day, Ben made a bamboo cage for the young egrets. That afternoon he borrowed Martin's wagon and rode out to Felt Gordon's. When Julie Gordon came out, he said, "I brung you a little something."

She looked at the birds, reaching in and stroking them and cooing to them. "Where'd you git them at, Ben?"

"I clumb a tree and got 'em. They ma was dead," he said, briefly. "I knowed how you like pretty things."

"Oh, Ben, I'm just ever so much oblige. I'll take the best kindly care of 'em," she said excitedly. "I'll be a new ma to 'em."

As he rode homeward in the dark, an uneasiness came over him. He wondered if he shouldn't have given the birds to Mabel McKenzie.

PART IV

Ben often wondered just
what went on in Blind Fiskus's head while his
fiddle sang alive with the quadrille music; his
face, hidden in the gray-and-black beard, was expressionless, and his dead eyes told nothing. Only
his fiddle and his nostrils seemed animated; they
said Fiskus needed no eyes, for he could identify
you by smell, like a yard dog. And his ears were
sharpest of anybody's. He never talked, or sang,
or beat his feet to the dance like the banjo player.
Fiskus was a basket maker by profession, but he

never worked at it until his whisky got low or he broke a fiddle string.

Now, Ben, wiping the sweat from his face with his red bandanna, watched the fiddler rather than the dancers, fascinated by the big blunted fingers that walked so cleverly across the violin neck. The dancers whirled, promenaded; the men were trying to shake the house down with their stomping, and near to doing it, and the caller's reputation was at stake as he tried to make himself heard above the noise — *big fat lady in the corner!*

Mabel whirled by, her eyes on her partner, smiling gaily, and by her bright manner toward everybody but him Ben knew something was wrong. Ordinarily he would have been anxious to discover the trouble and straighten it out, but tonight his inclination was to avoid her. He went outside, and the air was cool and, instead of cologne and hair oil, smelled of cape jessamine and the bright pepper string that hung from the porch rafters.

Ben sat on the rough, hand-hewn rail and swung a long leg disconsolately, puzzling over the peace he felt when in the swamp and the strange loneliness that held him now in the midst of the gaiety. He hummed absently to the music.

I wouldn't marry no crying gal,
And I'll tell you the reason why,
Her nose it's always dripping,
And her cheeks is never dry.

A shadow appeared in the door, and a girl came out onto the porch, fanning herself with a tiny handkerchief.

"Oh," Mabel said. "I didn't know you was out here."

"I am, though," Ben said.

"You git kindly warmed up in yonder," she said, with an ominous politeness.

"It's cool over here. The breeze can git at you."

She made no move to come closer to him. "This is fine right here, thank you," she said.

Ben stirred uneasily. "I ain't much in a dancing notion tonight, somehow another."

Mabel looked off into the night. "Guess it's because your girl ain't here."

"I thought she were. Er have you turned out to be Miles Tonkin's girl?"

Now she came over and stood beside him. "Miles treats me nice. He knows how to act."

"That's fine."

Mabel breathed deeply. "He don't go around giving a cage of birds to no Alabama girl."

"Ah, I just done it because she likes flowers and birds and stuff like that."

"Oh, yes, of course that was it," she said acidly. "It's curious to me how you found out what-all she likes, and you supposed to be a-courting me."

"Well, maybe you'd like to know how come I found out!"

"Not especially."

"I first went to see her the night the door was shut on me at my own girl's house."

"Well, I hope you don't expect me just to set and sew all the time you're monking around in that swamp."

"It's gitting where I don't expect nothing out of you but a bossified tongue and a cussing out. You act like both of us was married to each other except you."

"That's a nice way to talk," she said angrily.

"I don't guess Miles Tonkin would talk like that."

"No, he wouldn't. He's a gentleman."

"Well, why don't you git on back in there and do-si-do with him? He may like to be snapped at every time he turns on his heels, but as fer me, I got a gracious sufficiency of it." Ben had never been madder.

Her hand darted out like a snake, striking him sharply across the face. Ben drew back, and she slapped him again. He caught her wrists, and as she struggled against him, a voice said:

"You leave her alone, Ragan!"

Miles Tonkin, a big-boned, curly-haired boy, shoved in between them, grabbing Ben's arms. Ben twisted to meet him, thrusting Mabel out of the way.

"Now you'll git what's coming to you, Ben Ragan!" Mabel said shrilly.

Miles's fist thumped hard against the bridge of Ben's nose, blinding him and sending a spatter of lights through his brain. The other fist smeared his mouth. He tried to fight his way from the rail, but Tonkin held him there, battering at him with his bony fists. Now the blows carried no pain, only a numbed jolting. His legs sagged. Ben crumpled to the floor, trying to hold onto the rail. But he slid under it, and the ground came up and struck the back of his neck. The jar swept the light-sprinkled curtain away, throwing the scene into clarity. He saw Miles vaulting over the rail; behind him, silhouetted figures shoved through the dim-lighted doorway, asking, *Who is it? I don't know, somebody a-fighting. Tonkin*

135

and Ben Ragan, fighting over that McKenzie girl.

By the time Ben got to his knees, Tonkin was hitting him again, trying to batter him down. Ben's leg muscles bunched, and he launched himself into the other's belly, thrusting him backwards and off balance. Then Ben's fist cracked into Tonkin's face. The shock of it raced back along his arm and jolted his spine, clearing his head even more. Ben kept him facing the house so that the light made a white target of his face. Blood streamed from Tonkin's nose, then Ben's fist spattered it, two drops of it landing on Mabel's skirt.

Somebody grabbed Ben from behind, and he saw a pair of arms go around Miles Tonkin, and the fight was over.

Miles's eyes were glazed. Ben stood panting, his arms heavy, his tongue absently exploring a cut on the inside of his mouth.

"What started it, anyhow?" somebody asked.

Mabel said, "Me and Ben was just arguing. Miles didn't have no call to come butting in."

Ben looked at her. "He fit fer you, and he can have you."

He turned and pushed his way through the crowd, unmindful of the look of cold fury on her face. At the back of the house, he washed his bruised face in the well bucket, the water stinging the cuts and sprinkling pink upon the sandy ground. From the room the light notes of a fiddle came, as Fiskus sat alone and played, uninterested in the excitement outside.

Ben saddled Martin's horse and painfully mounted. Back at the house, he could still see them clustered around, discussing it. He turned the mare into the road, hardly knowing what he was doing because of the turmoil in his heart. The faint music of the fiddle followed him until he reached the woods.

Ben had made two more trips into the swamp before he saw Julie again. By now he and Tom Keefer had acquired five more new traps, and Ben had developed an increasing impatience for fall to be gone and trapping weather to come. This day he was keeping the store for Martin, who had gone fishing. The store was formally open only on Saturdays, but Martin liked to have somebody near by in case a customer came. Since he had to be close by anyway, Ben opened the doors and spent most of the day asleep on the rough counter. He was there when Felt Gordon came. Outside, Ben saw Julie, waiting in the buggy.

He hesitated, then called to her. "Git down and come in, if you're a mind to."

She came in, and stood admiring a bolt of factory-woven cloth while her father made his purchases. When Felt was through, he said, "I got to fix that crupper afore we start back. Ain't no use for you to stay out in the hot sun. I'll call you t'reckly."

Julie kept looking at the cloth, and said, presently, "One of them birds died. The other two is doing fine. They can fly and everything, now. Amos clipped they wings, and they live down in the creek right back of the house, where they can feed they ownselves. I named them Willie and Dora." Her eyebrow rose absently. "They're tame as a pair of dominicker chickens, and a whole heap prettier. I wouldn't take nothing for them."

"I'm glad to hear it."

Julie hesitated for a moment. "I thought maybe you'd a been back to see about them by now."

"I ain't hardly had the time."

She looked straight at him. "Ben, I heered you got into some trouble a while back. I hope you never got hurt."

"Not so bad that I couldn't git over it," Ben said, slowly. "I reckon you heered it was about a girl, too."

"Yes, that's the way it was told to me." There was a questioning look in her frank eyes that made him uncomfortable. For a fleeting moment he allowed himself to feel the warmth of her charm, and to think that no man could ever be dissatisfied with her. But he had felt that way about Mabel at first, too.

Ben took a breath, and said, with difficulty, "I guess she put an end to my courting days, unless I git a hankering for a bunch of young 'uns, sometime. I ain't no wise old man, and they's a lot of things I ain't straightened out in my mind, but I believe I got the woman business figured pretty nigh right. Soon as you commence a-courting, you're headed for trouble. If she don't care nothing about you, your poor heart's busted and you wish you had been dead-born. If she gits to be your girl, then first thing you know she's telling you not do that and you better do this, and how come you wasn't here before dark like you said you'd be. This here love, hit's just a big calaboose, except your food ain't free. There ain't but one way to git any satisfaction out of it; right after she lets you know she's your girl, if you'd walk straight out and put a pistol ball into your own head, you could fall over a-thinking, 'Ain't it fine?' and never know no better."

"A lot of people that's tried it don't think that-away."

"With all the people that takes the chancet, somebody's bound to turn out lucky. I just say it ain't a good gamble."

"How come you say it to me, Ben?" Julie asked.

Ben whittled on the counter with his barlow. "To tell the truth, I don't know. I just kind of had it on my mind."

From out front, Felt called Julie.

She kept fingering the cloth, but her eyes were on Ben. The yellow jackets hummed around a syrup barrel. She glanced at them and said, "I don't think I'll keep clipping them egrets' wings."

She turned and went out, leaving him puzzled.

Everybody said that Thursday Ragan was a changed man, but nobody knew why. He had not been fox-hunting since the night he fell into the stump hole and nearly broke his leg. Late in autumn he took his pack of hounds to his brother, Hardy, and said that he'd come back if he ever wanted them again. He never accepted a proffered jug any more, and from a friendly, somewhat boisterous man he had turned moody, and suspicious, and his friends felt that he was watching them.

"I don't know what's got into him," one of them said. "He makes me feel like my stock is eating his corn, or something."

It certainly couldn't be that he was putting more time on his farm, because the grass had ruined his peanuts, and his rail fences needed repairing, and you could count the ribs on his hogs. Neither could he have developed a new devotion for his wife, for on the few occasions when they were seen together, like at church, he never spoke to her, nor showed her any attention at all.

Even Ben was puzzled about it, until he went to see his stepmother late in November. Winter had come the day before, with chill winds in the pine tops, and morose, overcast skies, and this morning the cows found the troughs coated over with thin clear ice.

In the front room of the house, Hannah sat in front of a blazing lightwood fire, patching a quilt. Ben had left his new black traps on the porch, and now he slipped inside, and kissed her behind the ear.

"Who is it?" he whispered, holding her head.

"Couldn't be nobody but you, Ben, to come up and kiss me," she said, unhappily reaching back and taking his hair in her hands. "Where you been at, so long? In that swamp?"

"I ain't been nowhere. I was here just two weeks ago, er have you plumb forgot?"

"Two weeks is a long time."

"I'm heading for the swamp now. Got nearly all the traps I need," Ben said. "When winter's over, I'm goan git you a store-bought dress and a pair of little bitty red shoes."

She smiled at him, and mused, "Hit's good that I ain't got no boy of my own, cause I couldn't care as much about him as I do you, Ben, and that wouldn't be right." She stared into the fire. "Seemlike you're the only one I'm allowed to care about, anyway."

Ben asked, hesitantly, "How come you and him ain't hitting it off . . . er don't you want to say?" He had asked her many times in a roundabout way, but always she evaded.

"The reason I ain't told you, Ben," she answered, "is cause I been afeered you'd feel the way he does. I couldn't stand it if you got down on me, too."

"Go on and tell it then," he said uneasily, "if that's all that's a-holding you back."

"I cain't tell you, Ben."

"Is it something you done?"

She looked at him steadily, then said, "When Thursday was always fox-hunting, I used to git lonesome, Ben, a-setting here by myself, and wishing he was here with me, maybe not a-courting me, but just here, where I could look at him, er talk to him, er maybe touch him accidental-like. I thought some time another I'd git used to being lonesome, but it turned off worst instead of better. I used to set out on the porch and cry, listening to them hounds, and to the whippoorwills, and smelling the cape jessamine and the wisteria. One night a man come by, and we got to talking, neighbor-like. He come again, every time he heard the hounds and knowed Thursday was off. He weren't much, but he were better than nobody, and when he commenced to make up to me, I didn't put a stop to it." She glanced away, then looked back at Ben. "That night Thursday hurt hisself, he come home early, and caught us, only this man he run and Thursday never seen him good. That's what's the matter, Ben."

"Who was it that run?" Ben asked painfully.

She didn't answer him. "Ever since then, Thursday has turned bitter-like, and he don't go hardly nowhere, just sets around here, watching me, waiting for that man to come back. He don't eat what I fix for him, ner scarcely even speak to me, unless it's to try to make me tell him who it were," she said. "I got Thursday with me now, but I don't know but what it's worst than before. I cain't rightly decide where he hates me, er loves me almost outn his head. I've told him it wouldn't happen no more, but he won't listen."

Ben said nothing.

"He says I don't know my own mind," she went on softly. "He says if this man was dead he'd believe me; but as long as he's alive he's liable to come back, and that I'd have to let him."

For a long time Ben remained silent, staring into the fire. "I never reckoned it was nothing like that," he said finally. He stood up, feeling uncomfortable.

She studied his face, and then in a quiet voice said, "I knowed better than to tell you."

Ben moved toward the door, clumsily. "I reckon I better be gitting along, if I expect to be in Okefenokee today."

Hannah said, "I wisht I hadn't a told you."

He went out, leaving her gently rubbing the quilt with her fingers. Shouldering the string of traps, he opened the gate and stepped into the road. Through the window he could see Miss Hannah, still sitting there, staring at the quilt in her lap. As he stood, the chilled air crept through his two pairs of overalls and caused goose bumps on the fading brown of his skin. Down in the field, where Thursday was burning the grass and cornstalks, a billowing of white smoke climbed, and above it two hawks floated expectantly, waiting for the rabbits and rats to leave cover in front of the crawling red flames, the rats quickly, nervously, the rabbits puzzled and stupid, easy prey. The hawks liked the fires; wherever the smoke rose, they sailed above it with their shrill cries watching their good friend, the flame; knowing to plummet into any grass that stirred against the wind, knowing to cruise low above the cold-water branches, to whose damp fern-covered banks the puzzled rabbits clung, safe at last from the hot breath of the red fire, unmindful of the silent wings above.

Ben shifted the traps to his other shoulder, and turned down the road.

In the swamp, the alligators went to the hill to swallow pine knots to give their stomach something to work on during the hibernation. The snakes moved sluggishly, their eyes dull with cold. The otters, in their fine, thickening winter coats, fished in deeper waters with a new boldness, now that the gators had lost their hunger; and the bears no longer sought to besmear their hides with turpentine against the insects but explored empty logs and thickets for winter residences. Thousands of ducks — mallards and black ducks and sprigs and ringnecks — whistled in daily to join the gaudy year-round wood ducks.

As Ben drove his boat through the labyrinthine black water, the swamp was no longer green; the cypress needles were dead, and the maiden cane lay brown and dormant. Some of the birds had gone, and others had come; and the fur animals would soon be ready for trapping. Now, too, he and Tom Keefer could use Trouble in their deer hunting. This was the time he had anticipated all year, and now that it had come his mind was not on it, but on Miss Hannah, and the misery within him was like a disease.

Keefer waited for him on the edge of the prairie, still clad in his sparse buckskins. "I found more otter slides than we got traps fer," he said. "Ain't hardly no use to fool with coons, with all the otters' we can git."

146

"Ain't you cold with no more clothes than that?"

"Some. But I'll be used to it by a week or so."

"I brung you some warm breeches," Ben said.

Keefer shook his head. "I can stay warm, if I just put my mind to it." He rubbed Trouble's ugly head. "Now the swamp can listen to your big mouth, dog, and nothing to worry about, less'n you jump a panther that don't want to run, er try to dig a bear outn his hole."

As the cold continued, they visited the otter slides, thin, mud-slick pathways to the water, and buried the open traps just beneath the surfaces, unbaited. They baited a few traps for coons; on fox-walk logs they made simple wire snares, a sliding loop into which the fox, for all his cleverness, would thrust his head and tighten the deadly loop about his neck.

At night, after they had eaten, they built the fire up, because when they sat still they got cold. Tom Keefer said it was like trying to warm up the whole swamp. Sometimes the wind whistled in the trees with a mournful chill, and the limbs cracked together, and the fire seemed to squat closer to the ground, as if the devils of the swamp were stamping in it.

"On a night like this," Ben said, "I'd hate to remember I'd put a man under the ground."

Keefer watched the fire, and after a while he stood up and shrugged his buckskin garment loose so that it fell to his loin. On his belly was the eight-inch scar, light brown against the dark of his skin.

"You see that?" he asked. "I'll tell you about me and Katie."

When Mama died, I was just a lad of a boy, and Katie, she was just a creeper, as Papa called her. Papa wasn't fitn fer nothing fer a long spell afterward, just sat around with his jaws bunched up and his eyes mad-like, saying what a low-down trick God has sprung on him. I don't never remember him breaking down right out, he just stayed mad, and he'd stare at nothing; half the time he didn't never know we was nowhere about. He'd go out to plow, and wouldn't hardly git nothing done. I'd see him down at one end of the field, setting on that rail fence we built to keep the deers out, and staring out at the woods like they was somebody in there he was good a-mind to go and whup. I disrecollect how long that went on, but I know it were quite a spell. And all that time I had to see after little Katie. Just time I turnt my back, off the porch she'd go on her head, sometime not even cry, just crawl on under the house and start playing. I don't hardly know how she growed up, because I didn't have no idea about feeding no young 'un, and I give her grits and side meat and cornbread, just same as we had. And what little we had kept getting littler, only it took Papa a long time to see it. One day he looked around in the kitchen, and said:

"Tom, rations is a mite low, ain't they?"

And I said, "Yes, sir."

And that's all he said about it. And a while later, a week or so, he noticed again, and he said, "We got to git some something-to-eat in this house." But then he went on back out, like he was looking fer somebody to fight, and finally I knowed it was up to me.

That's how I stole my first pig. He belonged to that fellow down in the slough, I disremember what his name was, and it took me about all night to git him. I'd lay in one place an hour, and then crawl a little way and then be still another long spell. Finally I seen the shote I wanted; he was laying by the fence asleep, not fer from the house. I got close enough to touch him, and waited and

149

waited fer some noise to break out. After the last longest, the cow she let out a low, and by time it was all out of her I had that pig and out of the yard, with my fist rammed down his throat. When I got to the woods, I was so worked-up I couldn't hardly breathe. I hadn't never felt no such excitemint in my life. I guess the fever got in my blood right then. It were like hunting a bear or something, only more, cause a bear ain't likely to shoot at you. Once, after I had got onto the hang of it even more, a fellow got to telling a girl some lies that wasn't so about me, and I had to figure up some scheme to even up with him. I wanted to scrapple it out with him, but then I thought, she'll believe it more than ever then. So I stole another man's hog and turned him loose in this fellow's pen. I knowed he wouldn't go looking fer the man that belonged to the pig, he'd just keep him and say, well, well, look what come up with my hogs. And that's what he done. I was evermore'n satisfied with the fix it got him in.

When I brung that first pig home, I told them it was a piney-woods rooter I'd caught, and Papa he wasn't in enough of his right mind to notice that wouldn't no piney-woods rooter be all that fat.

Well, after while, Papa he sort of straightened hisself out enough to begin furnishing us, but whenever he'd sit down by hisself, he always had that mad with him, right up to he got kilt in the big mill. I got an idea he went to heaven with his fists balled up, and I don't imagine he was there more'n about two shakes of a goat's tail before God told him he could go straight to hell.

But even before he got kilt, it were me done the looking-after of Katie. She growed up like a boy, I reckon, cause me and her always fished the creek together, and hoed the field, and tended the stock. Oncet when she was about ten I caught her cutting out some cornstalk dolls, and she got mad at me for seeing her.

They was a boy named Jeff Somebody used to live about two mile from us, and him and me and Katie used to fish some. I believe what I'm goan tell you come about the same day Papa left to see about the job with the big mill that was putting up near Homerville.

"You ain't scared to take a-holt of things, Tom?" Papa asked me. I guess I was gitting along to where I thought I was full-growed, then. I said, "No, sir," and to tell the truth I weren't.

"Well, you see after Katie, and when I come

back I'll have cash money in my pockets." He did, too; but the mill finally got him.

This Jeff boy, he come along late that afternoon, and he said, "The cats are biting fine in the creek, let's spend the night down there and catch us a mess of 'em."

That suited me and Katie. She always did like to fish. You take a fishing woman, she's all right, she'll make a pretty good wife. Of course Katie was just a girl; her hair was gitting sort of a brown wave, though, and her eyes was light blue. You know generally a girl with brown hair's got brown eyes, but hers was light blue, and it give her a honest kind of a look. She were beginning to look like a she instead of a he, too, though I never noticed that right off. Fact about it, it weren't until way later, after she had married Josiah and begin to change, that I recollected what a playful, running-over sort of a child she had been. Always happy as a jaybird in a wild cherry tree, singing and dancing round; I told her oncet she should of been borned a nigger child.

She got some meal and coffee and stuff together while me and Jeff went down back of the lot for worms. You know how you drive a stob in the ground and then scrape acrost the top of it to make the worms come out. We took some pork liver too, fer bullhead bait, and a quilt to sleep on. We put the quilt on a sandy bend in the creek, and I went up the bank putting out set lines. That sand would sort of squawk when you walked on it. When I got back, Jeff had cut us some poles with the little short-handled ax we had brought, and Katie had a good fire going to run off the mosquitoes. We begun pole fishing, and before long we had some nice channel cat strung on the stick. Years after that, when I was hiding out in this swamp, I'd git to thinking about the way that coffee smelt that night on the creek bank.

After while we shuck the sand offn the quilt and stretched out on it, all three of us. But didn't none of us want to go to sleep, we just talked and cut the fool. Finally I said:

"About time to take a look at them set lines. Come on, Jeff."

"You go. I don't care nothing about no more fish," Jeff said dozy-like.

So I went up the creek bank and pulled in a mudcat and a eel and two empty hooks. When I come back on my way to the lines below the bend, I heard Katie say:

"Leave me alone, I tell you!"

I guess I never had much sense in them days. I thought he was just teasing her, spilling sand in her hair or something, and I said, "Quit bothering her, Jeff."

"Ah, I ain't doing nothing," he said.

When I come back, though, they was tussling, had done rolled off the quilt onto the sand, and all of a sudden it come to me the way Jeff had got up this idea, and then slept in the middle to be sure he'd be by Katie, and then wouldn't go work the set lines with me. Did you ever light a little pile of gunpowder and see the way it sort of catches and then *whoosh*, hit flares up all over? Well, that's the way this thing done me, I just went *whoosh* inside. If Jeff seen me coming — and I don't see how come he didn't hear that sand squalling as I run — he never paid no attention, just went on trying to hold Katie. I think he was plumb out of his mind, he was after her so hard.

My fist come down on the back of his head, and I never even felt no hurting, though it turnt out later I'd broke three fingers, and damn near broke his skull. That was the first sure-enough fight I ever had. God knows how I knowed to do all I done. After I hit him, I come up into his face with the top part of my bare foot. That sort of stunted him; he rolled away from Katie, and stood up, shaking his head. I come at him again, hitting at him, and coming up with my knee where it would do the most good. We fit some more, he wasn't as bad stunted now, and oncet when I knocked him down he got up slow. I seen he had that short-handled ax in his hand. Then, quick-like, he run in toward me, with that ax drawn around sideways aimed to chop me half in two at the belly-button.

I seen it coming, and I tried to jump backward; Katie screamed. I felt the ax snick open my clothes, and I figured he'd missed by a mighty close shave. Then Katie made some kind of a strangled sound, and I seen Jeff staring at my belly with his face white in the moonlight, and then he turnt and run. I don't never know what come of him. I guess he thought he'd kilt me.

And when I looked down at myself, I thought he had too. The corner of the ax had just nicked me, just enough to go through the skin. The cut was sagging open a little, not bleeding hardly a-tall.

Katie had stopped crying, now, and was on her knees, staring at my belly. I went toward her to help her up, and she yelled again, and I looked at myself and seen something was trying to fall out o' me. I pushed the gut back inside.

"Be still!" she said. "Don't move around."

"We got to get outn here," I said. "I got to have something another done to me."

"Who's to do it?"

"I don't know. Somebody."

"You can't walk. Everything you got'll fall right out o' that hole."

"I can hold 'em in."

But she made me lay down on the quilt, on my back, and not move. It seemed like she was gone half the night, but I guess maybe it wasn't so long. By the way she was a-blowing when she come back, she must a run all the way to the house and back.

She brung two needles and some white cotton thread, and a lamp, and a bottle of turpentine, and some bullet lead. She lit the lamp, and give me the lead to bite on, and then she sewed up that place with sewing thread.

She never cared nothing about the boys until she seen Josiah Wick. She had boys a-courting at her after she got big, but she never took none of 'em serious, just teased 'em and played with 'em like she was a boy herself. But when she first seen

156

Josiah Wick, a change come onto her. He had him the biggest, meanest horse in this country, and to tell the truth, Josiah could pure-out ride him. And he was a fine-looking fellow, like Jesse, as long as you didn't pay no attention to his eyes. They had too much white in them, like his horse's did. I always figured Josiah Wick's mean streak come from the Dorson in him. But I couldn't tell Katie nothing. She never lost her head, ner cut up like no kid girl; just quiet-like you knowed that she'd found her man, and she was going to love him if it kilt her.

Yes, and that's damn near what it done. I told her if she married him, her life would be ruint, and without batting an eye, she said maybe so, but if she didn't marry him she wouldn't even have no life.

Within a year she begin to see what I'd meant. She never bucked Josiah, tried to do everything just the way he wanted it, never talked back or sassed him. But seem-like that just brung out the mean in him more. You take a somebody like him, you behave decent and humble-like to him, and it just makes him worse.

Sometime she'd come to the house with red streaks on her back, and she'd cry, and ask me what she ought to do; and I'd tell her she weren't going back. But when I turnt my back she'd be gone again.

I don't crave to butt into no married people's business, but to tell the truth, hit had nearly-bout driv' me crazy, and I went to Josiah and I told him if he didn't ease up a mite, me and him was going to have trouble, and he said fer me to keep out o' his business. Why one time a fellow come to spend the night, one of his kinfolks, and before Jesus he tried to make Katie sleep with him! But she run out and slept in the woods.

When I finally had got a bait of it, I loaded up my gun and I headed for Josiah's house. I had it in my mind to call him outside and just cold let him have it. But when I got there, I heered her crying sort of loud, not yelling, and I knowed I'd caught him red-handy, and I kicked open the door. When he seen me with that gun, he jumped away from her to go fer hisn, and then's when I poured it into him. The hole them buckshot blowed into him, you could o' put a cat in. I ain't never had such a satisfaction in my life as seeing him rolling and kicking on that floor.

Katie didn't hardly seem to know what had took place fer a minute, then she went to Josiah and begin taking on over him, trying to hold him still, gitting bloodied all up. Then she finally looked up at me, and her eyes were flat-mad, like a panther cat's. She riz up and made a jump for Josiah's gun; and I knowed I better go, and I got out o' there. That same girl that sewed up my belly was wanting to blow it open again.

But I don't hold it against her. She done what she was meant to do. It's just like a gourd that grows on the vine. You cut it off, and it may end hanging to a chinaberry tree with a martin nest in it; or it may hang at a man's waist, full of gun-powder. Living er dying may be in it, but the gourd ain't got the say-so.

Several weeks later, when Ben started to the outland in his boat again, Trouble slept on a comfortable bed of furs, coon and fox and wild-cat and otter. The boat was heavy with them, and with venison, sun-dried and cured in sweet hurrah-wood smoke.

Just before he left, Keefer had stood on the bank on his long, knotty legs and looked at the furs, and said, "Now I can let myself think that it might be so, Ben. With the money from them yonder, and the rest we goan git, I can cross the swamp, and maybe find the St. Mary's, and go down it by night, and make it to Jacksonville. Some night I'll be long gone. I'll git me a job, and I won't be no outlaw, and maybe some good woman won't have no better sense than to marry me, and instead of dying in this swamp I'll go out in a feather bed with sheets on it, and my children and maybe grandchildren setting around, and not no buzzards er possums waiting and wishing I'd hurry it up. I'll think me up a good name, and live up to it," he mused. "Hit were a lucky day for me when you come into Okefenokee looking for that dog, Ben."

The next night, Ben went to his father's house, just after dark. He walked rapidly, impatiently, impelled by this thing on his mind that would not give him peace. He rattled the front gate, and shouted, "Hello!" and no challenging foxhound voices answered the call. The door opened quickly, and briefly silhouetted in the firelight, gun in hand as he stepped onto the dark porch, Thursday Ragan said sharply:

"I don't know who you be, but you stand right there, and if you move to run, I got something here what'll catch you!"

"My name's Ben Ragan," he said angrily, "and I ain't the running kind."

Thursday grunted and went back into the room. Ben walked up the steps. Thursday looked at him expressionlessly. "What's your business?"

"I come to visit Miss Hannah."

"She's back to the kitchen," his father said. "You ain't into no trouble?"

"I wouldn't come here if I was," Ben answered.

Hannah's face, dim in the kerosene light, was drawn and lifeless, a caricature of the handsome woman who had been his stepmother.

"How you do, Ben?" she asked, turning from the safe to look at him.

"I ain't much, thank you," he said, hesitantly. "How you do?"

She said listlessly, "I been wishing I were dead since I told you that, Ben, and you acted like you did. Not that it's in me to blame you."

"I never had no call to act like that."

"Hit's all right."

He struggled for words. "What I'm intending to say is, I don't hold it against you. Hit took some gitting used to, but now it don't matter."

"You ain't just saying that?"

"No'm, I ain't."

She smiled and moved toward the stove. "You had your supper?"

He was about to tell her that he had, but something in her eagerness stopped him, and he answered, "No'm, I ain't."

"I wisht you'd let me fix you a little something."

"I wouldn't want to put you to the trouble."

"Ain't no trouble," she said, and put the spider on the stove.

While Ben was forcing his second supper into his throat, and pretending to be nearly starved, Thursday came and stood in the doorway, watching him.

Thursday said, "I knowed you'd be back, begging fer something to eat."

Hannah said, "Leave him be, Thursday."

Thursday regarded her impassively. "You ain't been spoke to, ma'am." He looked back at Ben, who doggedly kept eating. "You still going in and out that swamp?"

"I'm making my living at it," Ben said.

"Cain't be much of a living, if you have to come here fer your something-to-eat."

"I don't have it to do. I just git a hankering fer some of Miss Hannah's cooking," Ben retorted. "You go down and take a good look at them furs I turnt in to Martin, and see what kind of living I'm a-making!"

"I told you to stay outn that swamp, boy. You never listened. Now when you leave here tonight, you stay left, you hear me? Don't come back fer no visiting, ner begging, ner nothing!" He glared at Ben, then went out.

Hannah put her hand on Ben's shoulder. "Ben, you'll have to kindly excuse him."

For once Ben was unable to be defiant. "I git tired of being cussed out by my own daddy," he muttered unhappily.

"You'll have to excuse him," she repeated. "Hit's partly on account of me, and partly them hogs that's being stole from him."

"What hogs?"

"Them range hogs. Every so often, somebody gits one of 'em."

"Well, hit ain't me a-stealing them."

"Hit's just heavy on his mind. Hit, and me."

The Suwannee is still an oversized creek when it crosses into Florida, black water, bordered with tupelo jungles in which cat squirrels bark and frolic. Jeb McKane's house sat almost in sight of it, and beyond, his field crawled up out of the lowlands into the palmetto flats. In the field a black man worked, burning and digging stumps, his

gray-black hands as familiar with the ax handle
as they were the paddles of Jeb McKane's wide
boats, and his voice drifting to the house through
the cold-sparkling air:

> "*Go long, Sal, nurse the baby,*
> *Go long, John, peel the taters,*
> *My old wagon is a-hauling corn,*
> *Way down in Florida.*"

Silas and Bud Dorson beached their boat on
the white sand of the riverbank, and climbed to
the house, where McKane sat in the sun in a homemade rocker, his hat pulled down over his brown
forehead. He was an enormous man with hardly
any belly; his eyes were dark and flinty; you
could never tell what went on in his head by looking at his face. He regarded the visitors unemo-
tionally, looking at them, then at the brindle,
shred-eared catch dog that followed.

"Howdy, boys," McKane said.

"Not much," Silas answered. "How you been,
Jeb?"

"Not much," Jeb answered.

"Been dry, ain't it?" Bud said.

"It has that."

"And cold," Bud said.

"Cold, too."

"We was just out messing around," Silas said, "and thought we'd stop and see how you been."

"You must a left fore day," Jeb said, glancing at the descending sun.

"Just about day."

"A little before," Bud put in.

"Come in and set a while."

"Don't care if we do."

They sat on the edge of the porch and talked about the weather and the crops and the hunting, and finally Jeb said, "How'd y'all make out at the feather-hunting last spring?"

"We made out good. We had us a time, afterward, too, didn't we, Silas?"

Silas's harelip widened. "We God shore did."

"Maybe you could lun me a little," Jeb said, unsmilingly, watching them.

"That money's long gone."

Bud rubbed the dog with his foot. The dog panted quietly, his wide, capable jaws in a half-grin. "How's your peanuts this year?"

"I cain't complain."

"Ours didn't do nothing a-tall," Bud said. "We'll butcher poor-tailed hogs this year."

"Didn't know you boys fooled with hogs and farming and such."

"We just mess around at it."

Jeb said, "I lost nearly all my hogs with the cholera. Expect most of my peanuts'll rot in the ground."

"Now that's a pretty fix, ain't it?" Silas said. "Us with hogs and no feed, and you with feed and no hogs."

"I could use a few hogs, if y'all wanted to git shed of 'em."

"We might be interested in letting you fatten a few on halves, though to tell the truth we hadn't thought much about it."

"I wouldn't be interested in no fattening proposition. I'd buy outright, if we traded."

"We'd hate to git shed of them, straight out, after all the work of raising them," Silas said hesitantly. "What you reckon you'd be minded to pay?"

Jeb thought a long time, and finally he told them. Bud and Silas said they couldn't afford to sell their hogs for a price like that. Jeb said it was the best he could do, and they could take it or let it ride. After a while, they said they would study about it.

As they were leaving, Jeb said, "What's y'all's hog mark?"

"Sometimes we use an under-bit, but mostly no mark a-tall."

"Well, don't bring none with over-bits er swallow-forks. I don't want no stole hogs bunched up around me," Jeb warned.

When they were in their boat, and the catch dog was asleep in the bow, Silas said, "Now he's a fine one. He knows good and well we wouldn't take no price like he named if them was our own hogs."

"Ah, he's crooked as a blacksnake," Bud grumbled.

Ben ran his hard legs into his copperas-dyed breeches. This done, he sat lazily on the edge of the bed, wiggling his toes a moment before pulling on his brogans, and anticipating the Sunday ahead of him. This was meeting Sunday, with preaching and singing at the Hardshell log church. He would have liked to see some baptizing today, but of course it was too cold. Maybe there'd be some interesting girls to look at; perhaps Julie would be there, but he doubted that. Mabel would surely be there; this was not a pleasant thought, for ever since the night of the dance, her attitude toward him had been unmistakably venomous.

Dressed, with his hair greased down and his brogans sooted, he went out into the winter sunshine. Usually he had Martin to walk to church with, but Martin had left three weeks ago for Savannah. Ben wondered idly where the storekeeper and his brace of oxen were now; were they still plodding through the trackless wire grass? Or had Martin reached Savannah and sold the furs and syrup and beeswax and even now had the cart loaded with the factory cloth and barlow knives and sugar and other replenishments of the store's meager stock? Next year, Ben thought, he would ask Martin to let him make the two-months' trip too, and he would get to see what a big town was like, and eat such things as oysters in one of those restaurants, and see a locomotive engine.

When he reached the church an hour later, the preacher was lining out a hymn. The place felt hot after his walk, although the stove was far from red. Almost against his will he looked to see if Julie was there; but she was not, nor were any of the Gordons. He sat on one of the rear board benches and let his eyes glance across the rail that separated the women's side from the men's side. A girl, Lucy Farhan, came in the women's side; and the eyes of the congregation automatically turned toward the men's door, where should appear Cliff Dekle, one of the few boys bold enough to bring his girl to church. A little high of color, Cliff came in and sat down and fastened his gaze studiously on the preacher, who was ready now to commence.

— *And on that Day of Reckoning, will you be There to see His shining countenance, can you say, "Lord, I'm only a sinner, saved by grace," er will you be in that other place, with your heart and soul on fire, a-begging to Good Lord to just please cool the tip of your tongue? Now's the time to make up your mind! Now's the time to git right down on your knees, and ask Jesus to come into your life. Hear me, people: don't delay . . .*

Ben listened, and stirred uneasily, wondering if the Lord would fall plumb out with a man for a little cussing and liquor drinking and an occasional visit with careless girls. He would have liked to ask the preacher privately about this, but knew he'd never have the nerve, especially since he and the other young folks were still in bad because of that dancing last summer. Tom Keefer, now, he had done a sight of thinking about such things, maybe he would know. Ben resolved to ask him, next time he went to the swamp.

The preacher read some from the Good Book, and Ben's attention wandered briefly. He noticed that Thursday wasn't listening at all, but was gazing speculatively from one man to another, and his calloused fingers drummed restlessly on the back of the pew. Across the rail, Hannah sat next to Mrs. Tulle McKenzie. The preacher paused until Fred Ulm got through putting pine knots into the stove.

After services, Tulle McKenzie called several of the men aside, and led them over to the edge of the clean-swept graveyard. Ben went curiously, filling his corncob pipe with home-grown rough cut.

"Boys," Tulle said, "hit's a fine meeting day, ain't it?"

"Shore is that."

Tulle looked at the ground grimly, and pushed at an acorn with his foot. "How come I called y'all off," he said slowly, his voice louder than necessary on account of his deafness, "is cause I'm missing another hog, and I been wondering if I were the onliest one."

"No," said old John Dekle, "you ain't."

"No," Thursday Ragan said, "you God shore ain't."

They talked of the missing hogs, and where they were last seen, and about their earmarks; but nobody had seen any of the lost stock.

"I hate to say it," Hardy Ragan muttered, "but it looks to me like we got a hog thief amongst us."

"Hit looks like it."

While the womenfolks at the church waited impatiently, the men talked, telling again how the missing hogs had failed to come up with the others, and how the next day had been spent searching; Tulle leaned in close with his hand on his ear, but by now the conversation was lost to him, and presently he said, "I'm like that drunk fellow at the beekeepers' meeting; when they was done, he roused up and said, 'Well, boys, what did we decide?'"

"We hain't decided nothing. To tell the truth, we ought to thrash this thing out when we got the time. How come we don't git together at Tulle's house this evening about two hours by sun?"

"We got to do something another," John Dekle said, angrily. "If I lose any more o' my pigs, my family ain't goan have meat to go on through the wintertime. Hit ain't just hogs that's being stole, hit's rations outn our young 'uns mouths — " the old man's harsh, outraged voice dropped ominously, and his watery eyes sputtered — "and let me tell you we shore ain't going light on no hog thief we git our hands on!"

That afternoon, Ben uneasily joined the group of purposeful men in Tulle McKenzie's living room. It was the first time he had been in that room since he had stopped courting Mabel. Everything in it should have been familiar, but it was a foreign place: the pedal organ with its faded fringed scarf, the marble-topped table, in the center of which sat the kerosene lamp with polished chimney; the cowhide straight chairs, the velours-covered brick doorstop. In another part of the house he could hear the footsteps of Mabel and Mrs. McKenzie as they made coffee. Much as he wanted to find out what the men would do, he wished he had not come.

Thursday had not showed up; Ben guessed that he preferred to solve his problem alone. John Dekle sat on the horsehair sofa, trembling with old age and indignation, and Cliff, his son, stood with an elbow on the mantel, probably with his mind more on Lucy Farhan than stolen hogs.

Patient Fred Ulm sat close to the fire. Blind Fiskus, who owned nothing worth stealing except his fiddle and two first-class hound dogs, had come, but had not spoken. Hardy Ragan had come, and Felt Gordon, and Clem Hooper, all of whom had lost stock.

"Mind you," Tulle said, "I ain't accusing nobody. But for argumint's sake, you got to think it's me a-doing it, and I got to think it's you. Now who you know of around here's got more pigs than they due to have?"

"Not me," John Dekle said. "I'm due to have more'n I got."

"That's me," Hardy said.

"They's been at least a dozen hogs stole," Fred Ulm broke in. "If they be in this section, they can be found."

"Maybe they been butchered," Ben offered.

"What you say, Ben?" Tulle asked, leaning forward.

"I said, maybe they been butchered."

"Whoever killed mine butchered poor hogs. Mine wasn't near fattened."

"Ner mine."

"Well," Ben said, "ifn it were me goan steal hogs, I'd wait until they was fattened."

Hardy said, "Maybe whoever done it were too hard-up to wait. And anyway, hit's easier to steal a hog when he's still in the woods than when he's rooting in a field. I say whoever done it has got every one of them hogs in a peanut patch somewhere another."

"Then they ain't within ten miles o' here," Fred Ulm said, "er somebody would know about it."

"That's the truth."

The door opened, and Mabel came in with a pot of coffee, and several cups and saucers. She served Ben last. "Sugar, Mr. Ragan?" she asked.

"Please, ma'am," he said uncomfortably, under the cold smile that reminded him strangely of her mother.

"Hit's a pleasure," she answered.

The men, except Hardy Ragan, watched them in amusement. Cliff Dekle winked viciously at Ben. Hardy poured his coffee into his saucer, blew it carefully, and said, idly, "I reckon if Tom Keefer were still round about, we'd have a pretty good notion who to go git."

"Now ain't it so!" John Dekle echoed.

Ben said, "Well, now, I wouldn't be too sure about that. Don't know as Tom Keefer would a stole a dozen hogs, one right behind the other. Maybe a fat shote now and then, just when he needed it."

They all looked at him mildly, a little startled that anyone would defend Tom Keefer, and Ben immediately wished he had kept his mouth shut. Especially when he saw that Mabel, in the act of going out, had stopped and was staring at him with curious pleasure.

"It's always been a puzzle to me," Tulle said, "where that fellow got off to."

"I always figured he somehow another made it to Jacksonville and caught one o' them boats. Though how he done it I cain't rightly say, with the word out fer him everywhere."

Mabel spoke boldly: "You don't reckon he's holed up in that Okefenokee Swamp?"

They regarded her politely. "Couldn't nobody made out in that swamp this long," John Dekle said.

"Well, they's *somebody* in the swamp that traps with Ben Ragan," she insisted.

She had their full attention now. Ben sat motionless, his hands locked tight around the chair rungs under the seat. The fire hissed. Somewhere Mrs. McKenzie's footsteps sounded busily. A coffee cup clinked in the room, and Felt Gordon cleared his throat. Outside a hawk screamed, and the muffled cries of the chickens drifted through the closed window. A roar grew in Ben's ears, accompanying a foreboding, a premonition of disaster. He sat transfixed, waiting.

"How you know they's somebody in the swamp?" Hardy Ragan asked quietly.

"Ben told me so, hisself!" Mabel said, shrilly. "He told me hisself — *said it was somebody they was after!*"

There was another long pause, and the only sound now was that of Mabel's excited breathing.

Fred Ulm asked, "What about it, Ben?"

Ben's voice would not come. He tried to grin, and that would not come either. Finally he managed to say, "Hit's just a fellow. A — a nigger."

"No it ain't no nigger!" Mabel insisted. "Ben said it wasn't no nigger!"

"I just told you that," Ben said weakly. "Just an old nigger, that's all."

"Hit ain't no nigger!" She dropped one of the cups. It smashed on the floor, and the handle rolled in wobbly fashion under a chair. Nobody noticed. "I been trying to figure out who it were, ever since that day Ben told it to me, and just then, when he said what he did, hit come to me! *Hit's Tom Keefer, that's who!*"

In the backyard Mrs. McKenzie shouted for Tulle to come with his gun right quick, there was a hawk after the chickens.

Old John Dekle rasped, "Ben, is Tom Keefer in that swamp?"

Ben stared stolidly at the wall, his mouth clamped shut.

Fred Ulm rose. "You heered what he said, Ben. Now answer him, boy!"

"I ain't a-saying," Ben snapped.

"If it ain't Keefer," Hardy Ragan asked, "then who is it?"

"Ask her," Ben said bitterly, nodding toward the triumphant girl. "She knows so much about it."

"We've done heered her. Now we asking you."

"Well you can just ask right on."

"Ben," Hardy Ragan asked, "is it Tom Keefer in that swamp?"

They waited. Ben didn't speak.

"Listen to me, Bud," his uncle said slowly. "Maybe you don't know it, but Tom Keefer done a murder; and if he's anywheres round about, the chances is that he's the one gitting these hogs. Now you want to help us out, er you want to stick by a fellow like him?"

Ben maintained his stubborn, red-faced silence. Mabel still waited by the door. John Dekle was standing now, bent forward, his hands shaking, mouth half open.

"We got to have an answer, Ben!" Fred Ulm demanded.

"I ain't a-saying," Ben muttered.

Fred Ulm straightened slowly. "Seem-like to me that's answer aplenty."

"Yes," Clem Hooper agreed, "if it weren't Tom Keefer, he'd a said so long ago!"

They all seemed of this opinion, and now the tight quiet was gone, and in its place came a restrained excitement; the men talked in pairs and threes, all except Blind Fiskus, who gave his entire attention to his coffee saucer. Mabel went out and got a broom and swept up the broken cup. Ben watched her with an emotion that was too deep for anger; she had gone out of her way to be treacherous, to break her word. That was the woman in her.

"Ben, you got to tell us whereabouts Keefer's at," Clem Hooper said.

"You done figured it out," Ben said angrily. "He's in the swamp. Now go git him. Ought not to be more'n seven or eight hundred square miles to Okefenokee. Borry you some boats and go find him."

"You'll have to take us to him."

Ben laughed with a savage bitterness. "That's where you're plumb mistooken. Go find him. I told you where he was at. In the swamp. Take you some bloodhounds — some you don't care much about, cause if you ever manage to follow 'em on his trail you'll find 'em dead. You've hunted panthers, ain't you? Well, Keefer won't be much worse, except that a panther ain't got no gun, and Tom Keefer won't tree," he told them. "He's in Okefenokee Swamp, just like that girl said. Go git him. If you hunt good and hard fer a month er two, and don't lost yourselves, er git wild-hog et, er timber-wolf et, er snake-bit, you might find him — if he don't find you first!"

"Ben," Hardy Ragan said harshly, "if Tom Keefer's in that swamp, we got him to go git. To-morrow."

"Well, go git him then."

" — And you got to go with us."

"I reckon I'll have a little to say about that."

Clem Hooper's voice was ominous. "I don't know as you will."

Ben stood up, watching them. Cliff Dekle stepped in front of the door.

"Don't git in my way, Cliff," Ben said.

"You're fixing to make trouble fer yourself, Ben," Hooper said.

Ben moved toward the door. Cliff Dekle spread his legs. "Don't git in my way, Cliff," Ben said again. He went around the table, so that it was between him and the others.

Fred Ulm ordered, "Let him on the outside, Cliff."

Cliff moved aside, his eyes expressionless. Ben walked past him, stiffly, and opened the door. They followed him out the hall, close enough to touch him. Ben thought to run, but Cliff Dekle was a fast man afoot, and even if he outran Cliff, he'd not gain enough distance to mount Martin's mare. In the yard, Cliff stepped in front of him again.

"I told you not to git in my way," Ben said, and threw his fist. It landed on Cliff's forehead. Cliff ducked under the second blow and grabbed him around the middle, shoving him back. Somebody else tried to pin his arms; Ben jerked sideways, and saw Fred Ulm go spinning into the dirt on his back. Now someone seized him from behind, and another pair of arms clamped around him. When he tried to kick, Clem Hooper grabbed the foot, and all of them went down, and they had him.

On the porch, Mabel stood motionless, eyes wide above her hands at her mouth.

"Go git that plow line yonder in the barn, girl!" Tulle McKenzie shouted.

But she didn't move, just stood transfixed. Ben writhed helplessly against the weight of them, trying to drag an arm free. A rough coat was against his face. He managed to draw his legs up a little, then kicked quickly, and for a moment broke the hold on them, but whoever was at his legs fell across them and they were pinioned again.

"You goan git that rope er not?" Tulle asked.

Mabel still did not go. Her mother came running up with the plow line. Although Ben fought, presently his legs were bound tightly together. They had more trouble with his hands and arms.

They moved back and looked at him, panting.

"What's he done?" Mrs. McKenzie asked.

"He ain't done nothing but be hardheaded. I guess we got to break him up of it. He knows where Tom Keefer is at."

"He always was mighty biggety."

They went off a way to talk. Now Ben could see Mabel standing on the porch, looking at him; and beside her appeared Fiskus, feeling for the steps with his foot.

Hardy Ragan came and stood over him. "Ben, you're my kin, and if you was in the right I'd stick by you. But you in the wrong."

"I don't need no help from you."

Clem Hooper came from the back of the house with Tulle's wheelbarrow, its homemade, solid-wood wheel creaking. They lifted Ben upon it and rolled him out of the yard toward the creek, a man on each handle, another walking beside to hold him in the wheelbarrow.

Finally at the edge of the creek, they laid him on the damp leaves of the bank, face down. The leaves put a sweetish dead smell into his nostrils, and out of the tops of his eyes he could see the transparent russet water.

"If you want to make it easy on yourself, Ben, now's the time to do it. It's only right that we catch that murdering, thieving Tom Keefer, and we got to have your help. We aim to have your word on it fore we leave here."

"You shore won't git it!" Ben told them.

"Ain't no use argufying with him. Put him under, Fred."

They moved him just to the water, holding his head up. Fred Ulm stood knee-deep, his face pale against the cutting chill of the creek. Ulm's hands closed about Ben's shoulders, and abruptly, before Ben could draw in his breath, shoved his head under.

The water was icy. It bit at the roots of his hair. Ben knew better than to fight even what little he could; but a ringing grew in his ears, and his lungs seemed about to burst. Instinctively he struggled, trying to twist his head toward the top. Panic grew within him. Ulm snatched him up suddenly.

Ben's breath came out in an explosive gush. Before he could suck in the new air, Ulm, timing it perfectly, thrust him under again. This time Ben's lungs were empty; air-starved, they seemed afire. The noise in his ears was deafening. *By God*, he thought in terror, *he's shore goan drownd me!* Now a star-burst of lights streamed through his brain. The blood hammered in his temples. Then he dimly anticipated that he was about to be brought up, and he opened his mouth to be ready for the air. Convulsively his lungs expanded, and instead of air he inhaled water. The water was like acid, strangling him.

Briefly he was up again, coughing, choking. Distantly, Fred Ulm's shout came to him, an imperative whisper: *You ready to say it?* Ben tried to speak, but before he could control his suffocated retching, he was thrust under again. Frantically he thought: *How can I tell him yes when he won't leave me out long enough?* He tried to yell, but the sound was only a muffled, agonized mumble.

"You ready?"

He realized that his head was no longer submerged. He tried to speak, but he only croaked and coughed. For a moment he was held there, the water running out of his hair.

"You better say something quick!"

Yes, yes! Couldn't they hear him? *Yes!*

A far-off voice said, "Give him a minute, Fred, he's trying to say something."

My God, ain't I saying it? Cain't you hear me?

"You better say something, Ben!"

For an instant the dizzy whirling slowed, and Ben's eyes focused. Fred Ulm's legs were close to him, the trousers limp in the water, dark-wet like a blotter from above his knees down to the water.

An inch below Ben's face the creek, the torturer, waited.

"You goan say it, Ben?" the voice insisted.

A spew of water came from Ben's open mouth. He fought the choking, and when he spoke, he said: "You cain't make me!"

Down his head went.

Gradually the dark terror subsided. In its place came a pleasant, anesthetic twinkling of lights, floating him. Trouble sat in the front of the boat, scratching his ear. A yellow fly lit on the side, preening transparent wings with its hind feet. Ears raised, Trouble watched the fly the way he watched the bees when he went to the woods in spring with Miss Hannah, to pick pink honeysuckle for the green-glass vase. The water rippled pleasantly.

Abruptly, Ben was dragged back. The damp leaves now were warm against his blue cheek; the sounds that drifted to him were insignificant. There was an angry roaring, the swishing of brush. Of the distorted scene, he seemed to see Fred Ulm floundering and gasping in the channel of the ice-water creek.

Now one of the sounds fastened itself to Ben's brain familiarly. Again the sound came, carrying a bull note, a note of fury, and suddenly he knew it was his father's voice. With an effort he half turned on his back, and saw a blurred Thursday Ragan standing almost over him, flailing those big red fists at anybody who would come within reach.

PART V

BEN's head still ached as if it were being squeezed in a cider press, but he noticed the smooth, clean bed sheets. He rubbed the palm of his hand back and forth; the pillowcase was warm against his face, not clammy and dead-mellow like the creek-bank leaves onto which Thursday, arriving late at Tulle's because his horse had gone lame, had dragged him. Ben didn't remember much about what happened; there hadn't been much to it, the men not wanting to make a fracas of it, although they probably could have handled Thursday even in his wild-bull fury. Ben recalled Thursday's oaken arm holding him up in the middle like a sack of grits, so that his head was down, and the water running out of his mouth and nose when he sort of coughed, and the burn of it in his nostrils. And he would never forget Fred Ulm bobbling in the frigid creek. Like flashes from a bad dream, he remembered the steadying grasp of his father's hand later, whenever he sagged sideways in the saddle.

"This ain't the way," he had once roused to say.

"You trying to tell me I don't know my way home?"

"I'm living on Martin's place."

"Not no more."

"I got something to say about it," he muttered.

"Listen, son," Thursday said dangerously, "don't let me hear no more outn you."

Miss Hannah brought his breakfast on a serving tray. He couldn't eat any of it. Miss Hannah finally gave up, and took it off the bed. Thursday came in while she was still there, but he did not speak a word until she left the room. Ben wondered how they managed to stay under the same roof. Marriage was truly a puzzle — a puzzle that he intended never to try solving. Mabel's treachery still appalled him; women were like cats — they were pretty and soft, but you should never forget they had claws.

"Well," Thursday said, "I guess you see the trouble your butt-headedness got you into. If you'd a minded your daddy and stayed outn that swamp, you wouldn't be in no fix like you're in."

Ben shoved himself up in the bed, and put his feet on the floor. His head whirled dizzily.

"What you doing? Lay down," Thursday said.

"If you'll hand me them clothes, I'll be taking myself offn your hands."

"You lay down, boy. You're sick."

"I ain't so sick I got to lay up there and listen to you give me down the country. I knowed that was all you drug me outn that creek fer."

Thursday's fingers drummed on the bed. Ben noticed that gray hairs had found their way into the dark red of his beard. "I drug you out because you was my boy," Thursday said, almost gently. "Like that fellow in the Good Book. He was a king, er something another, and his own boy tried to kill him. But they caught him at it, and when the boy he tried to run, his hair got tangled up in a limb, and somebody shot him, whilst he was a-hanging there. When the king seen it, he forgot the meanness the fellow had done him; all he recollected about was that it was his own boy."

Ben ceased to fumble for his shoes.

Thursday said, "Lay down, Ben. You're home. You and me ain't goan have no more disputes."

"That'll be mighty fine," Ben said slowly.

After Thursday had gone out, Ben lay back down, staring at the wall thoughtfully. To his surprise, a tear rolled out of his eye, and crawled across the bridge of his nose, and fell with a tiny thump to the pillowcase. He looked at the wet, transparent spot, and at the striped ticking of the pillow showing through.

The day when Ben rode off to breed Trouble to Whilsy McDonald's brood bitch, it never occurred to him that he would pass right by Felt Gordon's house, until he was within sight of it. He didn't want to stop. In the first place, Felt had been one of the men at Tulle's — not that Ben felt hard toward him, like he had thought he would. The main reason he didn't want to stop was Julie.

Ben planned to ride straight on by. Amos Gordon, though, was splitting cordwood at the side of the house, some of which he had already loaded onto the wood shelf outside the window. Amos straightened and held his ax across his legs.

"Howdy," Ben said, reluctantly stopping the horse. Trouble and the yard dog bristled at each other through the paling fence.

"Howdy," Amos answered. "Julie ain't home."

Ben almost answered, *Ain't that just too bad?* but caught himself. He said, "I was just passing on my way down the road a piece."

"Guess you might as well know it," Amos said, cropping the ax head to the ground. "She won't be home no more, leastways not when *you* come."

"Reckon that's Mr. Felt's doings," Ben mused, and put his heel into the horse's side. It solved a problem for him, but he still didn't like it. He guessed he was in bad with pretty nearly everybody, now, on account of Tom Keefer.

An hour later, on his way back, he saw somebody sitting on the rail fence that marked the beginning of the Gordon farm. The afternoon was warming up, but still it was not the kind of day one would select to be out, just to sit.

"I was in the house when you come by," Julie said. "I heard what Amos told you. I just wanted you to know hit weren't my idea."

Ben dismounted, and leaned against the horse's shoulder. "I reckon it's your daddy's idea."

She was looking straight at him, the way she always did; it unsettled him. "I heard about what-all happened to you, Ben."

"Looks like I'm always into trouble of one kind or another," Ben said. Curiously, he asked, "How come your daddy to out with a forbid like that? I ain't been up here more'n oncet er twicet, and he ought to know I ain't in the market for no new girl after the way the old one done me. I know hit's on account of Tom Keefer, but I ain't been a-bothering you none."

He watched the smooth line of her eyebrows. She was looking full at him again as she answered, "Hit were because he caught me crying, after I heard about what they done."

Genuine alarm seized Ben. "It weren't nothing to cry about."

"Oh, it wasn't because they hurt you, exactly. You ain't no small boy, to worry about. I guess how come I cried," Julie went on thoughtfully, "was just seeing you so stubborn and mad, and them a-trying to git something outn you. I could a told them they was wasting time." She smiled at him.

"You're a curiosity to me, Julie Gordon!" Ben exploded.

"I remember the day at the sing. I didn't like you a whole heap. I smelt whisky on you."

"You're apt to again, if you git around me at the right time."

"It ain't that. Only, I knew the whisky was what caused you to make up to me. Especially after you never come to the house but oncet er twicet afterward."

"I told you why I never, that day in the store."

"I ain't scolding at you."

Ben hesitated a moment, recalling the day of the sing. "Anyway, whisky never had nothing to do with it. I had just a second ago took that one drink when I seen you — it hadn't scarcely more'n hit bottom. A man don't git drunk until he's swallowed good."

"You're just saying that."

"No I ain't." He turned and pulled himself into the saddle. "Well, I better be rambling, I reckon. Don't guess I'll git to see you no more, long as your daddy feels like he does."

She looked directly at him, and said, point-blank, "You want to see me, Ben?"

"I wouldn't want you to right out and disobey your daddy."

"That ain't what I asked you. Anyway, since

when you been such a great one on the side of obeying?"

"I'm my own man, and I do like I please."

"I reckon now you've answered what I asked you," she said.

"Not yet."

"Yes, you have." Her long legs flashed over the rails, and she slid down on the other side. "Guess I better git on back myself. I told them I was after sedge for a yard broom. Expect when I show up at home I better have some, don't you?" She gave him a friendly smile, and was gone.

The Dorson boys and Jesse Wick were waiting for Ben Ragan, too. They sat beside the road, Jesse uneasily playing the guitar, Bud whittling, and Silas lying back and picking his teeth through the opening in his harelip.

"How come you reckon he's been messing around with such as Tom Keefer?" Jesse asked.

"Up to some devilmint another," Bud said.

Jesse sang:

> *"I take my guitar this morning,*
> *I pick it on my knee;*
> *This time tomorrow evening*
> *It'll be no use to me.*

"Papa, oh, dear Papa,
Your words has come to pass;
Drinking and bad women
Has been my ruin at last."

"I wisht me and Bud had a been at that creek," Silas mused. "We'd a got it outn old Ben Ragan, aye grannies."

"Hit ain't too late," Jesse suggested.

They looked at their cousin with amusement. "You mighty courageous-like, with me and Bud along."

"Don't fergit hit were my own brother that Tom Keefer shot," Jesse answered angrily.

"We ain't fergitting nothing," Bud assured him. "We'll find out where he is, one way another. When we find out, Jesse, you going in with us to git him? Er you goan let us tend to the fellow that shot your brother right by ourselves?"

"I'll be right there," Jesse said; he spoke without conviction, as the image of Tom Keefer came to mind, cunning and dangerous, a swamp creature. But his cousins would be with him, he remembered, and his confidence returned. "We've waited long enough for this gitting-even."

"That's the truth, all right," Bud agreed grimly.

They fell silent as they heard Ben's horse coming down the road at a lope, the sound of hoofs muffled in the sand. The horse saw them first and threw his ears forward. Ben pulled her down to a stop.

"Git down, Ben," Silas invited, "and kill a little time with us. Jesse was just playing 'Speckled Bird.' How you been?"

"Tol'able well," Ben answered, watching them narrowly. He noticed that Bud had casually stepped into the center of the road, and was stroking the horse's head. "How y'all been?"

"Cain't kick a-tall. Ain't you goan git down and be sociable?"

"Shore wisht I could, but to reach home by dark, now, I'll have to ram a cucklebur under this horse's tail."

"We aimed to ask you a little something about Tom Keefer," Bud said.

Jesse Wick concentrated on his guitar, playing nervously, not glancing up at Ben. The horse shifted its feet.

Ben said meaningly to Bud: "I wouldn't stand in front of this horse if I was you. Sometimes she jumps straight ahead, sudden-like."

Bud stroked the long, ugly head, smiling. "This horse knows better than to run over me."

"What was it you wanted to ask Ben about Tom Keefer, Bud?" Silas asked, interestedly.

"I heered you knowed right where he was at, Ben," Bud said.

"You did?" Ben said.

"Shore did. Is it the truth?"

"No," Ben said. "Right this minute I couldn't rightfully say where-at he'd be."

Annoyed, Silas said, "You know where-at he mostly stays, though, now don't you?"

"Yes. In the swamp."

"Whereabouts in the swamp?"

"On an islant."

"What islant?"

"Hit ain't got no name, that I know about."

"How'll we find him, if you don't tell us nothing?"

"You just go into the swamp and keep monking around, and maybe in a week er so, somebody'll open up and begin shooting at you, and if you live long enough to git curious about it, that'll be Tom Keefer."

"Maybe we'll have something to say about that shooting."

"Tom Keefer'll know you're in the swamp two hours before you see him. If you ever see him a-tall."

Their little black eyes were flashing now like sparks from an anvil, and Ben knew it was time either to fight or to get going. When he spoke again, the jeering note in his voice had been replaced by a businesslike tone. "Bud, I told you oncet not to stand in front of this horse. Now I'm fixing to go, and you better move to one side."

"Don't be in such a hurry," Bud ordered. "We ain't through talking with you." He slid his hand under the bridle and closed his fingers. "Now let's see you run her on over me."

Ben kicked the mare. She jumped sideways, and swung around the grinning Bud, flicking her tail nervously.

"Ain't you gone yet?" Bud taunted.

Ben jerked back on the reins, and kicked the mare savagely. She seemed to explode beneath him, rearing, and lifting the diminutive Dorson a foot off the ground. He dropped free and rolled frantically out of the way.

"Damned if you ain't a pretty good old horse," Ben laughed admiringly, as the mare pounded swiftly down the road.

Next day, he started into Okefenokee, the news he had to carry Tom Keefer almost weighting him down. He left Trouble at home.

After the sun came up, the day turned warm. He stopped and rested for a few minutes, and ate a piece of the cornbread and pork sausage he had brought. Long before noon he was in the swamp, now poling, which was easier, the boat whispering against the pickerelweed and never-wet leaves.

A lone poor-joe bird rose from a screen of bay bushes, squawking in outrage, and circled, and flew back along the trail of upturned bonnets and disarranged grass that Ben's boat had left. A little way farther, a bunch of about fifty black ducks got up and turned south. Watching them, Ben saw the poor joe settle, far down the run.

He would have forgotten the big bird altogether. But in the next moment, faintly he heard the bird squawking again. The sound registered in his head without meaning, until with a start he realized that the poor joe had again been flushed. Looking back, he saw the distant bird above the water oaks and cypresses.

"Somebody," Ben thought, "thinks to follow me to Tom Keefer. They'd a damn near done it, if it hadn't been for that old poor joe."

Whoever it was stayed far enough back to be safe from sight, yet close enough to make use of the temporary trail Ben's boat left through the watergrass and bonnets. Ben let his stob pole trail in the dying wake of the boat in indecision. The winter sun now shone down warmly, reflecting in the black swamp water, casting shadows of the gaunt bald cypresses. A cooter climbed upon a snag and basked. A tremendous flight of green-winged teal, perhaps a thousand of them, came hurtling overhead, bringing the sound of taut canvas being whipped by a wind as they split and flared up at the sight of the boat and man.

Ben watched the swift little ducks as they re-formed and went on; then they were out of sight, but he kept watching, and presently they appeared again, flaring into sight above the trees. Ben was positive, now, that there was another boat.

On impulse, he turned into an inlet. Then he paused, glancing at the position of the sun to get his bearings.

"They goan be took on a walk they won't never quite git over," he thought determinedly. And he added, as an afterthought, "Ner me neither."

It would have been helpful if he had known just who was following him. Possibly it was Fred Ulm and Cliff Dekle, or some of the other men who had lost stock. Or it might be the Dorson boys, and in that case he had a hard day ahead, for Silas and Bud were good woodsmen.

"Just to be on the safe side," he thought, "I better figure on it's a-being them."

He landed his boat, and pulled it up into the brown maiden cane, though not so far that it wouldn't be noticed. With him he carried the knife and his gun. He stepped out of the boat, and sank to his knees. The apparently solid earth around him undulated.

Slogging his painful way across the marsh, he began to sweat, and his nose ran. Convinced that he had left enough trail to be followed easily, he began to make use of the roots and cypress knees and log litter as steppingstones, and the going was somewhat easier.

Ben could not be sure that they were following him, but he had to take that for granted. If he waited to hear them, or see them, he might also be seen himself, and that wouldn't be safe, especially if the Dorson boys decided he was trying to lose them. They were not above shooting him in anger and worrying about their own fix later..

After an hour, Ben's curiosity almost got out of hand. Were they following him, or was he traveling across the badlands for nothing?

Gradually he drew closer to a vast thicket of hurrah and pin-down bushes. He kept heading toward the thicket, changing his course to enter the bays of it, hoping to find an opening through it. By now his legs were almost lifeless with lifting through the bogs, and he was covered with cold mud to his chin, where he had gone down in a sinkhole. As the afternoon grew, a few mosquitoes gathered and followed him, attacking steadily.

"Whoa," Ben muttered suddenly, stopping. The thicket had closed in on three sides of him. Either he had to try to pierce the jungle ahead, or turn back. If he turned back, he'd likely meet his trailers. If they were the Dorsons, the thicket, he decided instantly, was much the better alternative.

The hurrah bushes were bad; the pin-downs were enough to drive a man crazy. The hurrahs were simply thick; but they had a pleasant odor, and in spring small pink flowers, and the wood was good for meat-smoking. The pin-downs had nothing to recommend them. The original stalk grew out of the water, slender and reddish and sparse of foliage; its branches bent down to the watery earth, and wherever the tips touched took root, making a snare to catch a man's foot, and sent up new stalks, all of which developed branches that also bent down and took root, forming hoop after hoop. There was no end to it.

Ben wiped the mud from his knife handle and attacked the thicket, lunging at the pin-downs with a touch of panic. For, once in the thicket, his followers — pursuers, they were now — would have something of a ready-made trail, while he had to sweat for every inch. He fell often, splashing in the cold dirty water. The hurrah and titi bushes struck at his face, and the hoop bushes tirelessly ensnared his legs. Upon a charred cypress stump that rose like a rotten tooth, he climbed to look back. Not a hundred yards behind, the brush was in movement. They were close.

Ben assaulted the jungle, cutting where he had to. When he fell now, a lassitude came over him, and he had to fight his way out of it and get up. The thicket gave way with an infuriating slowness.

Ben hacked at a tenuous vine with the dulled blade, missed, and went down. He started to raise himself, then looked up. Directly ahead of him, not six feet, was the end of the thicket. Beyond high land waited, with palmettos and swamp pine trees, and an honest, solid earth for a man's feet. Seeing this, Ben allowed himself the luxury of a brief rest, lying there on his belly, his fingers locked in the damp roots. A water snake upon a slender branch watched him indifferently.

Ben rested longer than he had intended. Suddenly the voices came quite plainly, and he could even hear the splashing of feet. Ben got to his knees. Now he could see the bushes stirring, back along the trail he had made.

Quickly he wriggled away from the trail, shoving under the pin-downs on his belly, like a gator. The water snake dropped upon his back and slithered into the water. Ben crawled a few yards farther, then, almost submerged, turned to watch.

Now the splashing was loud, and he could hear their grunting. Through the brush he made them out; they were little men — the Dorsons. Ben held his breath.

"Look!" Silas said, stopping. "Yon's an islant!"

"Thank God we're through this mess," Bud panted.

"Just be still a minute," Silas said, lowering his voice. "That place yonder would be a mighty pretty hideout for Keefer."

They stood motionless for a while, peering through the brush at the high land.

Bud said, "I don't believe Ben Ragan would come and go through this thicket every time. If he did, he'd have him an old trail." He leaned down and picked up one of the last pin-downs Ben had hacked in two. "Look at thisn; hit's right fresh cut."

"Maybe he missed the old trail."

"Er maybe he knowed we was behind him."

"How would he a found that out?"

"I don't know the answer to everything, Silas, for God's sake."

Stealthily they pushed their way through the remainder of the thicket. As their splashing grew faint, Ben breathed easier, and rose. The water dripped from him noisily, and he sank again.

Finally he crept out into the trail. Again he waited, listening. A good-God woodpecker sped overhead, yelling shrilly. Slowly Ben started back out the way he had come.

Tom Keefer squatted like an Indian on the other side of the fire. The tree felt good against Ben's aching back.

"You ain't told me how come you showed up in such a fix," Keefer reminded.

"They's several things I ain't told you," Ben answered uneasily, "that's got to be told."

Keefer sucked fish grease from his fingers, and stood up. The fire made a shadow of his gaunt figure, with hard, slender legs, and long, rope-muscled arms and hollowed-out face.

"I reckon I might as well come right on out and tell you," Ben said.

Keefer waited. "Come right on out then."

"Well, a good while back, I had me a girl, and I told her oncet that I had me a trapping partner in the swamp. I don't know why I done it, unless'n it was because I was so crazy about her I never had good sense. Well, we had a falling-out, me and her, and I guess she got it into her head I had done her a low-down trick, and she aimed to git even. When somebody around there got to hog-stealing, they was a mention of you. And when they got to talking about you, and wondering where you was at, right then this girl guessed it was you I'd been a-trapping with. They put me in a creek, and damn-nigh drownded me, but I never told 'em no more." Ben concerned himself with pulling the dead bark from a stick, crumpling it in his fingers.

Presently Keefer mused, "And you was the one that was going to keep quiet so big."

"I was so set-up about us a-trapping, I guess I

just had to tell it to somebody," he said miserably. "Next time I'll have better sense than to let it be a durned woman."

"I should a known better than to let you go back out," Keefer snapped.

"You know they cain't never catch you in this swamp."

"That's so, I reckon." He squatted again, staring into the fire. "I expect you've done put an end to my gitting out to Florida, though. The word'll be out for me again, and just when I think I've made it, some sheriff another'll put a gun in my back and say, 'I know you got better sense than to run, Keefer, but I wisht you'd try it.' My grave'll be right yonder under that sycamore, like as not, instead of some floweredy graveyard."

"I guess I've done fixed you up proper," Ben said slowly.

After a while, Keefer said, "Well, I don't know. There wasn't no chancet of gitting out fore you come; and they ain't much now. Hit's about the same all the way round, I reckon. Maybe even better, cause you and that hound dog has been more company than the owls and panthers. Only, if I hadn't a never met up with you, I wouldn't a got started thinking about no new life, and maybe a little farm and a wife of my own, and such."

"They's something else got to be told. Silas and Bud Dorson, they followed me. I went ashore, and lost them, and the last I seen they was a-plowing straight acrost toward Bugaboo Island."

"They won't never find no way out," Keefer objected.

"What I ought to do is let 'em parish right where they're at, but I'll go blow 'em out tomorrow. I figure one night o' being lost will give them a gracious sufficiency of Okefenokee and we won't be bothered no more with them."

They smoked, and then got wood enough for the night. The wind was dead, and some of the warmth of the day lingered, so that it was not much like a winter night at all. The owls began their hunting.

"From now on," Keefer said thoughtfully, "me and you ain't goan have this swamp just about to ourself. You keep on a-hauling furs outn here, and sometime another they'll be more trappers to come. That's who I got to watch fer. I ain't scared of nobody coming in here a-hunting me; I'm scared of the fellow that'll run up on me when he's strictly a-minding his own business."

Ben said painfully, "I guess you'll be uneasy

about what'll come outn this big mouth of mine, too, from now on."

"You ain't goan give me up, Ben," Keefer answered.

"You don't sound very certain about it."

"How certain you want me to be?" Keefer asked quietly. "I'm depending my life on it."

By dark, Bud and Silas Dorson knew they were lost. They had crossed the tiny island, then retraced their steps, searching for Ben's trail, and not finding it.

"It beats me where-at he got off to," Silas said. "We know he come through the thicket."

"This ground's too hard to take a track. He left it somewhere, and that's the place we got to find. I just hope we run up on that scoun'l!" Bud said furiously.

They were convinced, now, that Ben had led them into the swamp and deliberately left them. Bud made a lightwood torch and moved slowly along, bent over, looking for tracks in the muck. A water-filled depression caught his eye, and he knelt to examine it. At first he thought it was a dog's track; then, with a prickling of his scalp, he realized that it was the track of a timber wolf.

He whispered, "Silas, look a-here."

There was no answer. Bud turned. The fire-light cut away the shadows. Close at him lay a huge cottonmouth, head lifted, the light reflecting on the white neck. Now the head drew back slightly, and the ugly mouth suddenly opened. Bud shoved the torch straight at the gaping, cottony mouth, and leaped away.

"Silas!" he shouted.

The other's voice answered from a palmetto clump, and Bud ran, not looking back to where the torch lay sputtering in the mud.

"We cain't leave here tonight," Bud panted. "Hit's too warm. I just seen a monster cottonmouth. I reckon the swamp's full of 'em, come out frog-hunting."

Silas rubbed his hand across his brow. "If we tried to find our way out tonight, we wouldn't never be heered tell of again."

Not far away, a panther screamed, the high-pitched, agonized sound of it sending shivers down their backs. Even the frogs stopped chirping and croaking for a moment.

Silas said thoughtfully, "He sounded like he was on this islant, somewhere."

"We cain't stay here," Bud said flatly.

210

"That panther won't bother us."

"I seen a wolf track too, fresh."

They went back to the clearing, both of them shaking and jumpy. Finally, with a big blaze going, they began to think about sleep. Then a new sound appeared in the menacing night. A savage, graveyard howl — timber wolves. After a while, they heard rustlings in the leaves just outside the firelight, and shadows moved in the flickering semidarkness. Now and then the light would catch a wolf's eyes, and glow in them.

They threw more wood on the fire and listened to the whispering feet beyond the palmettos. They sat with their guns across their laps and did not speak.

Long before morning, the wood began to give out. Neither of them mentioned it. They scratched around close by for twigs, and before long were reduced to putting leaves on the fire.

"If one of us don't git some wood," Silas whispered finally, "that fire's going plumb out."

But neither of them went for wood. They scooped up more leaves. Silas pulled small pieces of bark from the pine tree. But the fire died lower and lower. The furtive darkness crept closer.

They watched the fire.

When the last embers began to fade, and the darkness seemed about to grasp them, they climbed into the water oak, uneasily, wondering if a wildcat shared the tree with them.

At daylight next morning, the wolves were gone. They descended stiffly and left the island, heading again into the thicket. For an hour they floundered aimlessly, trying to find their way. But the swamp all looked the same.

An osprey circled over them and lit in a slender tree, his sharp voice echoing from the far-off cypresses, creating a sense of vastness, of emptiness; the swamp was a lost world; a nether land where the crawling things in the muck and the screaming things in the air had triumphed, and man rotted in the peaty earth; the space was the space of eternity, endless, changeless; a thousand years passed, and another thousand, and another, and man's bones were ground to ash by the ages, his gun a discoloration of rust beneath the earth. The osprey half opened his wings, then dropped over the side of the limb, leveled off over the shallow water, then rose again, and screamed; and the sound echoed and re-echoed across the flat swamp.

Silas suddenly stopped. He turned his head to one side. Bud, his mouth slack, stared dully at the bubbles that rose from around his brother's feet.

"Listen!" Silas panted. "I heered a horn."

Bud lifted his head. "Let's go to it then."

"We don't know who's doing the blowing."

"Don't make no difference, Silas, for Lord's sake, whoever's a-blowing is standing on high ground or a boat!"

They started again, moving toward the distant sound, their strength renewed by its note.

The blast of the horn was repeated. They tried to hurry toward the sound of it, floundering and falling in the muck, cursing, panting, trying to hurry before the blowing stopped.

But the blowing continued, patiently, at regular intervals. In another hour they were close to the sound, not more than a quarter of a mile. As they drew nearer, they slowed shrewdly, to reload their guns. But all the powder was wet.

Not that it mattered, the way it turned out. The horn blew no more; and when they reached their own boat, they were still alone. A depressed triangle in the brown maiden cane, with the grass just beginning to rise into place again, and a faint, slowly settling silt in the water, showed that another boat had been there and recently gone. On the bow of their own boat, a fresh-cut arrow-shaped stick pointed west, the direction from which they had come yesterday. They knew what the stick said.

They started poling, southwest.

Ben unloaded his hides onto the counter of Martin's store.

"Take them things out o' here, Ben," Martin said.

Ben looked at him, puzzled. "I brung them to sell, Martin, same as always."

"Take them out, anyway."

"What's wrong with them hides?"

"I can smell Tom Keefer on them."

"Oh," Ben said slowly. "I had figured that you was one man wouldn't hold nothing against me."

"I studied it out, Ben. They're right and you ain't. That's about all I got to say on it. If you aim to have truck with such as Tom Keefer, aim to sell his hides some'rs else."

"Where else?"

"Take them to Savannah, er Jacksonville, like I have to do."

"You know I ain't able to do that."

214

"Well, you'll have to git them out o' here."

It was night when Ben got home. He told Thursday, "I thought it was bad at first, but every way I turn it gits worse."

Thursday sat close to the fire, hands cupped toward it; his face was expressionless, his eyes distant, out of focus, and Ben knew he had been thinking about Hannah. Finally he said:

"I don't see how it can git no better, Ben, long as Keefer keeps up his hog-stealing. The Dorson boys went in to find him, and nigh parished gitting out, and Fred Ulm and Cliff Dekle tried it a couple o' weeks later, and got lost and nearly went crazy. Everybody has got better sense by now. I reckon Keefer knows he's safe, and does like he pleases."

"What would he do with them pigs that's been stole, anyway?" Ben asked angrily.

"I ain't got no idea. But it's curious to me that no time after the stealing starts, we find out Tom Keefer's close by. I know you ain't in on it, Ben; I think he's even got you fooled."

"He ain't stealing no hogs!" Ben said. "I'd know it if he was, I reckon. I got a little sense."

"You'll be saying he never killed Josiah Wick, next."

"Shore he killed him! You'd a too, if he'd a been abusing your sister."

"Yes, but that ain't what his sister said."

Ben opened his mouth, then slowly closed it. What Katie Wick had said was the barrier. She had claimed that Josiah, her husband, had caught Tom stealing a hog, and that Tom had shot him. She was right there when it happened, and Tom was her own brother; there had been no call to doubt her word.

Hannah came to the door and said, "Supper."

Ben rose. Thursday, as always, sat where he was, not having eaten his wife's cooking since that night he came home with his knee hurt, and a man jumped off the porch and ran. After they were through, he would go in the kitchen, and fry eggs and side meat; during the day, like as not he wouldn't come home for dinner, but would unhitch the mule and walk down to the clearing and inspect his rabbit traps, and if he had been lucky, he'd skin the rabbit and roast it. But he had not grown fat on his own cooking; his cheeks and shoulders were scooped out, and he belched whenever he sat down.

That night the sound of hounds drifted through the crisp air. Hannah had gone to bed, and Ben and his father were waiting for the fire to finish dying down.

"Listen at 'em," Ben whispered. "That's a stomp-down good race they're having."

Thursday was already listening. His head was up, and in the firelight his eyes were hot. "Hardy let on they was going to run tonight."

"Nobody said nothing to me about it," Ben said. "Reckon I know how come."

They listened. Now the hounds were closer, their voices pouring across the field.

"Let's me and you slip out and go," Ben said fiercely, "irregardless."

"You go," Thursday said, shortly. "I stay round here at night."

"No. I guess I better not go if they don't want me." He went out into the back yard, where Trouble sat tensely on his haunches, looking toward the hound song. Ben stood beside him. Trouble rose, went around Ben, and sat down again, listening.

Ben said, "Don't reckon *you've* got to wait for no invitation," and slipped the rope off Trouble's neck. The dog ran a way into the darkness, then returned, and whined at Ben. "You gitting mighty polite in your old age," Ben said. "Go on!"

Trouble went.

After a while Ben realized that the night was cold, and he built a fire in the back yard, and sat beside it, warming his hands and listening for Trouble's voice to join the chorus. Presently he heard it, a resounding bass note among the tenors; he pictured the hunters looking at each other in astonishment. *Dog if that don't sound like Ben Ragan's hound a-baying yonder. Shore does. Yes, sir, that's him fer true; they ain't no mistaking that note!*

Ben stood and turned to warm his seat. The back door opened and Thursday Ragan said, "I thought I heered old Trouble."

"Unless your ears was stoppered you shore heered him," Ben said.

Thursday came down and stood beside the fire, listening.

"That old gray's a-leading 'em on a run, now ain't he?" he said. And in a moment he murmured, "Yes, sir, they're into a pure gallop tonight!"

The sounds grew fainter as the fox began his wide circle.

Ben stared at the fire, and said, thoughtfully, "You reckon what ever come of Josiah Wick's widow?"

Thursday, intent on the hounds, turned to

218

look at him. "I heered tell she's living away from here, above the big mill, with a cousin o' hers." He shoved a stick into the fire with his foot. "Listen yonder. He's cut back on 'em, shore'n hell."

"He better cut back," Ben said absently, "less'n he wants that big-mouthed old fool of mine to run plumb over him and stomp him to death."

The man and his wife were stringing palmetto cords through the leaders of the hams, ready to put them into the smokehouse, and the stooped woman with the thin brown face was stirring the ash lye and cracklings in the pot with her battling stick, when the men got there. Four of them had come, Thursday, Ben, Fred Ulm, and Cliff Dekle. They spoke to the man and his wife, who watched them as they strolled hesitantly to the woman at the soap pot.

Thursday said, "Morning, Mrs. Wick. How you been, ma'am?"

She stopped stirring, and looked at them, and finally she said, without interest, "It's Thursday Ragan, ain't it?"

"Looks like we caught you at a busy time," Fred Ulm said, diffidently.

"Just making soap," she said.

"We come to tell you, ma'am," Cliff Dekle said boldly, "that we got a line on your brother, Tom Keefer."

She stared at him. "You've caught him?"

"No'm, we ain't. But we wanted to git something another kindly straightened out."

Ben watched her uneasily.

She said, "What was it?"

Cliff hesitated. "Don't know as we ought to be bothering you with it."

"With what?" She was stirring again now, automatically.

Ben said, suddenly, "I been with Tom, ma'am, and the way he tells it, he done what he did that night to keep you from being hurt."

"Tom was caught stealing," she said.

Fred Ulm glanced at Ben, then at Cliff Dekle.

Ben insisted, "Excuse me, ma'am, but before, nobody didn't think to doubt your word on it, and they was some things wasn't never asked. Fer one thing, if Tom was caught hog-stealing, how come the shooting was in the house?"

"It won't in the house. It was in the yard. I told them that."

"They was blood in the house."

"I drug him inside. I told them that."

Ben hesitated. She remembered her version of

220

the shooting too well. The other men looked at him impatiently, a little angry that he should keep bothering the woman with the things she was trying to forget. He recalled Tom's recounting of the shooting, and suddenly he lied:

"How come, ma'am, if the trouble took place in the yard, they's two buckshot in the front-room wall of what's left of that house?"

She looked at him, frowning. "Them? They — they come through the window. Er the door."

"They was too close together to've come far — more'n ten feet er so." Then Ben said gently, "You ain't treating Tom fair, Miss Katie. He told me he done it for your sake, and he ain't never lied to me yet. Said he done it to keep you from gitting hurt any more."

She stiffened. "I never asked him for no help! He didn't have no call to come butting in. Sometimes I went to him and cried about it some, but only because I cared for my man so!" Her voice had lost its dull tone. "I didn't want Josiah kilt. He wasn't no perfect man, but a woman's heart ain't her brain." The fire in her voice faded. She bent over the pot again, her face averted.

"Tom done it account o' the way your husband was doing you?" Ben asked.

"I never asked him to do nothing," she said,

stirring the pot dully. "Now I ain't got nobody. I don't want Josiah to be dead. I wisht he was alive. I wisht he was here right this minute — a-laying it onto me, if he was a mind to. I could a stood that. But seem-like I cain't hardly stand not having him."

"We just wanted to find out how it all come about," Thursday said.

When they were away from the house, Fred Ulm said, "Looks like she fergot herself and told the truth about it. I feel kindly sorry for her, but if it had been my sister, I reckon I'd a done the same thing Tom Keefer done."

A turkey gobbler hung from the peg on the side of the sycamore tree, its beard waving slightly in the wind.

Tom Keefer said, "I was hoping you'd show up pretty quick. Look yonder what I shot us. I yelped him fer an hour and a half before he'd come out." He threw a sycamore ball at Trouble. "And they's an old buck been fooling round here just begging some hound dog to come and see could he catch him."

Ben couldn't wait to say it. "Well, you better git your swamp hunting cleared up, because it ain't goan last much longer. I never come to do no trapping this time; I come to take you outn old Okefenokee fer good."

Keefer asked, "Just what you speaking about, Ben?"

"We went to see your sister. She told it straight this time. They ain't goan hold that shooting against you no more."

Keefer's hand closed on the front of Ben's sweater. "You wasn't never one to joke much, Ben," he said harshly.

"Hit's the God's truth. They ain't blaming you fer it."

"You mean I can just up and go out o' here?" he demanded.

Ben explained carefully. "Just about it. Only you got to keep a-going. Here's the way it is. They know you stole many a hog, and plenty of them got the notion you're still at it. But they know they won't never in the world catch you at it, ner git up with you in this swamp. So, if you're a mind to, they goan let you come out, providing you'll promise to keep right on going and not never come back."

"I'll shore promise that!"

"They want you to admit to hog-stealing, too,

2 2 3

so they can have that on you if you ever try to come back."

"I ain't never coming back. If I git to south Florida, I'll start me a new life all over again, and trade around until I got some land, and a good woman, and a garden with taters and collards and such. I ain't coming back. But if they want me to, I'll admit I done it. You can tell them that."

"They goan have to hear you say it out of your own mouth," Ben said.

Keefer studied for a moment. "They want me there myself."

"That's right."

Keefer said slowly, "They's a trick in that, Ben."

"They ain't no trick."

"All they want is to git they hands on me, one way er another!"

"You must be crazy. This is my own daddy I'm talking about. And Fred Ulm. And Felt Gordon, and Martin, and the Dekles. They're the ones that said it. If they word ain't no good, then the word of the Holy Bible ain't."

"Good men can be tricky, when they think good'll come of it in the end," Keefer said. "No, I ain't going."

"You listen. I been right with them men. I took them to see Widow Wick. I know they aim to let you go, without no trouble, and glad to be shed of you. All you got to do is tell them you ain't coming back, and admit what you done," Ben said with heat. "Don't you reckon I'd know the truth about my own daddy, fer God's sake?"

Keefer took the turkey from the peg and began picking it. The coon, now almost grown, stole one of the black wing feathers and crept away into the brush to hide his booty, while Trouble watched him thoughtfully. As the gobbler emerged from its bronze-and-black raiment, Tom Keefer said:

"Ben, they ain't talked you into nothing?"

"No they ain't!"

"And you think they aim to let me go?"

"Shore they do."

"You be certain of what you say. If you turn out to be mistaken, I'll be the one to pay fer it — with a cut throat."

"You must be crazy," Ben said, hotly. He went to the boat and brought out a bundle of cotton clothes and a pair of brogans. "I brung you these. Somebody might shoot you fer a varmint in what you got on."

PART VI

JESSE WICK sat on the porch steps of his sister's house in the dark. His back was against the post, and the guitar thrummed resonantly, and he sang.

> "*I rolled and tumbled all night long,*
> *Not no slumber did I find*
> *With that poor dying girl*
> *A-running through my mind.*"

Presently from her bed his sister called. "Jesse, I wisht you'd finally git a bait of singing and come on. We cain't go to sleep."

"I'll be in t'rectly."

He sang for another hour.

"Jesse, you coming er not?" Florella asked.

"In a minute."

"Ain't you froze out there?"

"I'll be on in after while." He started again.

Florella nudged her husband, worriedly. "Lem, slip out there and see if you cain't git his guitar away from him."

Lem got up and opened the porch door, but Jesse heard him and went out of the yard. Lem returned and got into bed. "He run off just like he done last night."

"I don't know what's got into him."

They listened to his voice from down near the fence, singing one song after another. Then for a while he was silent, and it was during this silence that the dog began to bark, and somebody came on the porch. They thought it was Jesse until Silas Dorson called.

Florella roused. "Now you reckon what Cousin Silas wants, this time o' night?"

Lem lit a lamp, and Silas and Bud Dorson came in, bringing their guns.

"Where's Jesse at?" Bud asked.

"He's out yonder. Listen."

228

Jesse had begun singing again.

"I never seen such a man for singing," Florella's husband said. "Last night he sat out yonder in the cold and sang plumb till daylight."

Silas asked in disbelief, "You mean he set out yonder in the cold and sang all night long?"

"That's what he done. And today about an hour by sun he started it up again, and he's been going it ever since."

"Well, call him in here. By tomorrow night he'll shore enough have something to sing about," Bud Dorson said.

Florella went to the door and called him. Jesse kept singing, apparently not hearing. She called again and again, and finally stopped.

"Jesse, will you for God's sake shut up and come here?"

"In a minute," he answered from the darkness.

"Come on now. They's somebody to see you," she insisted.

"You just want to git my guitar away from me," he retorted.

"Don't nobody want your old guitar," Silas called. "Come in here. We got something to tell you."

In a few minutes Jesse came in, blinking, holding his guitar close and watching them suspiciously.

"We got news about Tom Keefer," Silas said, his eyes sharp.

They looked at him quickly. Jesse wet his lips.

"Last night Bud went courting that woman that lives on old John Dekle's place. You know what they're aiming to do? They goan let him go."

"Let him go?" Jesse asked.

"They went and talked to Josiah's widow, and she told it that Keefer killed your brother on account of the way he was treating her, and they aim to let him leave the swamp and git away from here. Ben Ragan was supposed to go into Okefenokee today and tell him, and Thursday Ragan and Fred Ulm and Cliff Dekle and them goan meet him in the morning and hear him say he done some stealing and won't never come back."

Bud said angrily, "But we goan have something to say about that!"

"What y'all goan do?" Florella asked.

"That's all right what we goan do. We know the way Ben goes into the swamp, up the river, and he likely comes out the same way."

"When you going?" Jesse asked.

"Right now. We ain't taking no chances on being too late."

"You aim to spend the night in the swamp?" Jesse demanded.

"Not all the way in it. Just up the river a piece a couple of miles fu'ther up than where them others think they goan meet Keefer and Ben Ragan. They tried to keep it shut up, but I guess we're just a mite too sharp for them," Silas said. "We figured you'd want to go with us, Jesse."

"I'd shore Lord love to," Jesse said hesitantly, "but I'd sort of halfway figured on seeing a fellow about a cow."

Silas and Bud looked at him scornfully. "That's just with you," Bud said.

"That fellow'll be mad if I don't show up."

"You do just like you damn please. If you don't want to help tend to the man that shot your brother, hit's plumb all right with us. We don't need no help noway."

"That fellow won't like it a bit if I don't show up, but I'd shore like to help fix Tom Keefer proper," Jesse said, with a show of anger. "You wait. I'm a-going."

"We figured you'd want to," Silas said. "Well, hurry up and git ready. We got a long way to go."

*　　*　　*

Tom Keefer had put on the clothes Ben brought him, while Ben cooked breakfast.

"I never slept hardly none," Keefer said. "I got to thinking about how fine it's going to be. I still cain't hardly believe I ain't goan be no swamp man no more, and have a place of my own, and a wife."

The first faint light of day had begun to creep, and the thrushes whirred as they moved under the bushes, and the squirrels began to bark, and a great flight of waterfowl, ducks and geese and whistling swans, went overhead. There came to Ben a sudden regret, now that Keefer was actually going. From now on, he and Trouble would do their hunting and trapping alone.

He said, "I can make out why you're set on having a place, and a shore-enough bed, and no sheriffs after you, but how come you want to marry some woman is something I ain't figured out."

"Now that ain't no sensible question."

"That ain't what I got in mind," Ben said. "You look at my daddy, that don't even eat what Miss Hannah cooks, ner have nothing to do with her. And look at Tulle McKenzie, happy cause he's finally turnt deef and cain't listen to his wife devil at him. Marrying may catch some folks, but I thought you'd a had better sense."

Now the darkness was almost gone. An owl flew overhead silently, headed for his roost and sleep.

"I've had time to do some thinking on it," Keefer said. "It ain't that ache in your bones that calls for gitting married. This world's a lonesome place, mostly, with folks listening but not caring. You don't matter a whole heap to nobody but your own kinfolks, and not much to most of them except your papa and mama and your wife and children. But when you start gitting old, your papa and mama they'll be dead and gone, and your children they'll be busy with they own living, and the only one that'll care where you're at and what you're a-doing is your wife. Might be she hates you, like you say, but how you're gitting along is still on her mind. Hit ain't no bargain, being married, I don't reckon, but being single and by yourself ain't neither; and I figure if you was to line the both of them up side by side, being married would stick out just a mite."

Now the chill day had come, and the swamp rang with bird cries; a hollow tree vibrated with the clangor of a woodpecker. They shoved the boat off into the water mist that hung like wood smoke above the prairie.

Keefer stopped poling for a moment, letting

the pole trail, and looked back at the camp, the palmetto shack, and the coon that sat upon the stump and watched them indifferently.

"You act like you hate to go," Ben said from the front of the boat.

"Well," Keefer said slowly, as he started poling again, "the swamp hid me, and fed me." He nodded ahead. "I don't exactly know what waits fer me out yonder. But I reckon I can handle it. I'm shore glad fer the chance to try."

The sun rose, and Ben spelled Keefer at the poling. A warmth began to be felt; a rice bird lit upon a bladderwort stem. Distantly came the booming of a whooping crane, and a dark swamp rabbit stopped upon a sphagnum bog to listen. Now they had reached the great cypresses, and the wood ducks rose and filtered into their thin branches; and above them a flight of snowy egrets wheeled.

Ben watched the egrets, and remembered his feather hunt with the Dorson boys, and the three young egrets he had given to Julie. She had been proud of them; he recalled the flush of pleasure on her face. Now that he had begun thinking of her, he remembered her sitting in the buggy at the sing. The buggy had been unhitched, and she had not much liked the way he had made up to her. He remembered her queer, independent eyebrow, and the flash of legs when she swung over the fence the time she came to tell him that her father's disapproval of him had not been her doing. At the moment, he had thought she told him that because she liked him, but now it occurred to him that she might have done it because he had brought her the egrets.

"If Felt Gordon fell out with me on account of Tom Keefer, like everybody else done," he thought, "I reckon he'll kindly have to fergit it, now that Tom turnt out to be in the right about the shooting."

After an hour, Tom Keefer again took the pole. Now the lake was narrowing, and the cypresses became runted; and the banks were thick with titi and bay. A doe, heavy with fawn, watched them briefly. Trouble stood up and whined eagerly.

"You whoa, sir!" Ben commanded, grabbing the dog's tail.

The doe swung around on her hind legs and crashed away through the thicket.

Keefer said, "I'm shore goan miss that dog, Ben. Guess I can find plenty to hunt in Florida, and somebody to hunt with me, but it won't be the same without that old hardhead along."

Ben was silent a moment, then said, "I'd like fer you to take the old fool along, if they was another one like him, but I wouldn't hardly know how to do without his devilmint. If I knowed where you was goan be at, I could try to git one of his puppies to you."

"When I find me a woman that ain't particular who she marries, maybe she'll be good at writing, and I'll send you a letter. Sometime another you can come down to see me. Expect they'll be a bunch of kids around by that time," he said.

The day wore on. Flying low above the water, wing tips almost touching, a water turkey came up the river. A big bass whirled at a roach, making a dimple upon the black water; and near the brushy banks the smell of bream hung. At every bend of the stream, river ducks got up with a drumming and a splashing, to circle high around and light back down after the boat passed on.

In the deeper water of the Suwannee, they paddled instead of poling; and the growing current helped. A somber quiet seemed to have settled upon the river, so that the only noise was the dripping of the water from the paddle blade.

"I'll spell you," Ben said.

Keefer did not answer. His eyes were looking downriver, sharp. Now he did not paddle, but held the blade edgeways in the water, guiding the boat while he sat alertly upright.

"What's the matter?" Ben asked.

Keefer looked at Ben speculatively for a moment, then said, "They's something ain't just right. Hit's too unnatural quiet. And we ain't seen no birds since we made that last bend, not even no ducks."

Ben studied the river ahead. It was surely quiet, now you noticed it. A soft-shelled turtle rose to watch curiously, then silently descended, leaving a mild boil upon the surface. Other than the tiny gurgle of the water about the bow, there was no sound. Ben felt an indefinable uneasiness. Then a bald eagle rounded the bend ahead of them, his great wings flashing with the morning sun.

"Look a-yonder," Ben said. "If that old eagle's been messing around here, no wonder they ain't no ducks on the river."

Keefer began paddling again. The river unwound again, and for a short way ahead was straight, the black deep water of the left bank latticed by water-oak roots and sand vines, and on the right the red-amber shallow water shelving to a white beach. They passed a tiny creek that joined the river.

The roar of the gun, coming upon the deathly silence, was deafening. For a split second paralyzed, yet Ben saw the great puff of black-powder smoke from the screen of palmettos on the right bank; and he knew somehow, by the sound of the bullet or by a quick backward glance he never remembered taking, that the paddle handle across Tom Keefer's chest had been shattered, and juniper splinters driven into the swamp man's face and shoulders. In the next second they had both gone overside, the boat rocking violently, then quieting and floating on downstream sideways, carrying their guns, with Trouble looking back curiously.

Ben had dived deep, and the icy water hurt his loins as he swam, and finally the soft bottom rose beneath him. He came up against the left bank, half screened by the down-hanging roots. Keefer's head emerged quietly, like a gator's, just above him. Ben peered through the roots toward the right bank, but nobody was to be seen. He guessed whoever had shot was reloading behind the palmettos.

Directly above them, a voice said, "I'm looking right down this barrel!"

They glanced up to see Bud Dorson's face against the side of his gun, and the gaping huge muzzle not five feet from them; Jesse Wick appeared beside Bud, a short-barreled derringer in his hand.

"Climb out," Bud ordered.

Keefer and Ben Ragan pulled themselves up the bank with the aid of the roots, the sand clinging to their clothes. The faint breeze against their wet bodies was chilling. Bud and Jesse Wick watched them, Bud's face set in a cold mask, his eyes bitter and fierce like an osprey's. Jesse's eyes sparkled brightly.

On the other side, Silas had walked down to the beach.

"I guess you thought you was goan get away with it," Bud said vengefully.

Keefer's hardened face turned toward Ben Ragan. "Where I made my mistake," he said softly, "was not cutting your throat that first time."

Silas called, "You wait till I git there, Bud!"

"You had your chancet," Bud said.

"You better wait."

Bud turned to Jesse Wick. "Shove the boat outn that creek and go git Silas."

Ben heard Jesse's feet, breaking twigs and crackling the dry leaves as he made his way along the shadowed bank toward the hidden boat.

Bud looked at them appraisingly. "You better drop them sheath knives on the ground," he said.

"Might as well not have mine," Keefer said matter-of-factly, as he drew his blade out. "She wouldn't cut cheese."

Ben had forgotten, since that day he had fought with him beside the pond, how quick Keefer could be. Even before he had innocently finished complaining about his knife, the swamp man jumped inside Bud Dorson's gun. With his left hand holding the barrel tight, he rammed the sheath-knife blade into Bud Dorson's chest. Ben heard the slight scraping sound as the blade was twisted against the ribs. Dorson sagged and fell, his fingers clutching spasmodically at the dry leaves.

With a faint redness on the knife, Keefer whirled toward the other bank quickly, and dropped just as Silas Dorson fired. The bullet struck the brush and whined away. Keefer glanced threateningly at the frozen Ben, then, crouching, ran in the direction Jesse Wick had gone. Ben crawled around a clump. Jesse had stopped to see why Silas was shooting; now, with the derringer in his pocket, he turned to see Tom Keefer bearing down upon him with a blood-stained knife.

He stood there, mouth hanging open. Not until Keefer was upon him, knife drawn back like a striking cottonmouth, did Jesse Wick move. Automatically, much too late, he raised his arms defensively. The knife fell, and he croaked hoarsely and toppled forward. Keefer shoved the boat out of the little creek, swinging sharply to hug the right bank. The paddle flashing, he stooped low and sent the boat cutting through the black water.

From across the river, the desperate metallic pounding of Silas's ramrod electrified Ben. Quickly he crawled to the twitching body of Bud Dorson, which lay across the rifle. Disengaging the dead man's hand from the trigger, he rolled the now bleeding body over. Then cautiously he raised the gun, and looked across the river.

But Silas had jumped back into the brush, and was probably now ramming home the lead intended for Keefer. Looking down the long barrel of Bud's rifle, Ben watched for a movement in the brush, wondering if Silas was in position to see upriver.

Still no sign from the other bank, except the clank of a ramrod. Then a roar, and a cloud of black smoke drifted away. Ben stood up quickly, afraid of what he would see; but Tom Keefer still paddled steadily. The boat crept around the bend and was gone. From the other bank, Silas swore.

"Bud?" Silas called presently, still hiding. "You all right?"

Ben said, "No, he ain't all right, Silas. There ain't nobody but me and you, now. Both boats is gone, and we're a right smart piece into the river swamp. Hit's complete to my liking, Silas; after this day's work you've did, I got a little settling up to do with you. Ain't but one of us goan live to walk out of here."

"Hit suits me," Silas snarled.

Then Ben saw this slight movement; something vaguely round showed through a thinning of the leaves. Ben lined his sights on the faint silhouette of it; and just as he squeezed the trigger, it occurred to him that the thing was the powder gourd that hung to Silas's belt. The heavy recoil of the gun threw him back, but above the ringing in his ears he heard Silas's angry shout.

"Too bad you never reloaded fore I blowed your gunpowder to hell and gone," Ben said grimly, ramming a new charge into his own gun. "Now I'm coming at you."

He worked hurriedly. Silas would have to run — probably was already running. Catching him would not be easy, because Silas was a man of the woods. Ben robbed Bud's body of the powderhorn and shot bag. As he moved toward the bank, he remembered the derringer. He turned back to the little creek, where Jesse Wick lay face down.

Ben lifted Jesse's hand out of the way, then suddenly dropped it, startled; there had been a pulse in the limp wrist. Jesse Wick was not dead. Ben swung the gun around. Was Jesse trying to trick him?

Cautiously Ben eased the body over; it had the rubbery limpness of death. And the mouth, half-filled with trash and earth, hung open like a dead man's. Yet the pulse was there. Ben tore open the red-soaked shirt. The wound, a long slicing gash from the bottom of the throat to the right short ribs, wasn't half enough to kill a man. Ben rose, and hesitated momentarily, looking down at him, puzzled. Leaving the derringer, he ran to the riverbank.

Holding the heavy gun and the powderhorn precariously above him in his left hand, he shivered violently and slid into the water. The river bore him placidly around. He fought the quiet current, swimming with his right hand. Just when he thought he had made it, his foot struck a snag and he floundered, and went under, gun, powder and all. Ben swore through cold-blue lips, dropped the stuff, and swam toward the opposite bank, quartering into the current.

Trouble came rushing toward him from somewhere downriver, his white-and-red coat still damp from jumping out of the boat at the sound of the guns. Ben stood knee-deep, and stared at the eager dog, struggling with a sudden idea. He waded out, stripped off his water-heavy sweater, and tore a length of cloth from his shirt tail. This he bound around Trouble's mouth to keep him from baying.

"Never tried you on no man scent," Ben muttered, "but now's a mighty fine time to try it!"

With another cotton strip he made a short leash; this would keep Trouble trailing close, and

244

also keep his head up so he couldn't claw off the muzzle.

Ben led the dog into the brush, where Silas had been hidden. There was the gun, and an empty whisky bottle, and the tiny pieces of the shattered gunpowder gourd. Ben held the gun close to the dog's nose. Trouble, annoyed at the cloth on his mouth, showed no interest. Ben said "S'git 'im!" and stuck his nose into a footprint. At once Trouble came alive. Ben led him in a circle around the spot. Suddenly Trouble stuck his nose at another footprint; his neck bulged as he tried to bay, only a throaty rumble issuing.

"S'git 'im!" Ben encouraged, and the hound turned away from the river, following the hot trail of Silas Dorson, and half dragging Ben along.

By midafternoon, Ben knew that Silas was a fast traveler. From the look of his tracks in occasional soft ground, he was going at a trot.

Ben's clothes were still damp, but he had forgotten that he was cold. When the trail turned back toward the river, he stopped briefly in disgust. He should have known that Silas wouldn't risk getting lost in the river flatlands, and sooner or later would head back to the Suwannee; if he had thought of that, they could have traveled easily down the bank for a few miles, and waited for Silas to come following the river.

They again were at the river, far below the scene of the ambush. Now Trouble dragged hard, and again tried to bay, and Ben guessed that at last they were getting close to their man. He stopped briefly, watching. In that moment Trouble got his claw into the cloth that bound his muzzle, and suddenly he let out a note that reverberated through the river swamp.

Ben grabbed him. "Now you've done it, with that big mouth!" he said, replacing the cloth. "He'll know I'm right in behind him."

Any tree or titi bush now might hide Silas Dorson, waiting to spring out like a rattlesnake. Ben drew his knife.

A drove of black ducks came up the river on whistling wings; in the distance sounded the whine of a bobcat. A slender snag bobbled in the current. They crossed a slough that emptied into the Suwannee. Trouble's hasseling became feverish. Abruptly Ben stopped. There was blood upon the ground.

Puzzled, Ben went back to see what had happened, and found on the bank of the slough the jagged piece of limestone that must have laid open Silas's foot. "Now I guess we got him," he thought exultantly.

Farther down, the visible trail turned into the river, on the shallow side. Trouble tried to swim out but Ben held him. For several minutes he squatted there, trying to study it out. He stared at the stain. What had Silas done? Certainly he hadn't swum on down the river, for no man could stand the chill of it more than a few seconds. If he had crossed, Ben could follow him, but he wanted to be sure. If Silas had gone in and come back out on the same side, was he now below, or had he waded upstream a way and hid beneath a bank while they passed?

Again Trouble tried to get into the river. Curious, this time Ben sent him on. The first thing the dog did was claw the cloth off. He swam out a way, then turned back in toward the shallower water; and suddenly he bayed furiously, the sound ricocheting off the water and echoing through the woods. Ben followed down the bank. Now Trouble lost the slender scent upon the water. Holding his nose high, he swam in circles, and he straightened out downriver again, mouth going.

Then the dog emerged, dripping, too excited

to shake himself. In the damp sand the bloodstain showed again. The plain trail led into the woods. Ben caught Trouble's leash.

As he straightened up, something fell upon his hand; and it was dark in the dusk, like pitch. Trouble boomed frantically. While Ben stared at his motionless hand, startled, another drop of blood fell upon it, and another. He moved back, and above him, high in the upper fork of the sweet-gum tree, was Silas Dorson. The little man sat there silently, looking down malevolently, like a panther. In his hand the naked blade of a steel knife glinted faintly.

"Looks like we've treed you."

"You got me to come git, Ben Ragan," Silas said ominously.

Ben pulled off his sweater. "That's what I aim to do!" he answered.

But it was not the way he would have preferred it. He'd rather have fought Silas anywhere than above him in a tree. *Wisht I'd a had an ax*, he thought as he pulled himself up to the first branches. *Or a gun*. Silas had evidently counted on not being found, but he couldn't have selected a better place to make his stand.

Five feet below Silas, Ben stopped and looked

up. Silas was squatting in the fork, monkeylike, holding on with his left hand, and leaning down with the knife. Ben tried to study out the best way to attack, but there didn't seem to be any best way. *Don't look like I can go up without gitting stobbed. Might count on trying to catch his hand, if it wasn't so dark.*

"Come on!" invited Silas, beckoning evilly with the knife.

Ben moved up: and immediately the knife whispered viciously just above his head.

"Just a little fu'ther," Silas begged.

Ain't no way but to take a chancet, Ben decided. *He cain't kill me in the head, and he cain't git to my throat, ner hardly stob me in the heart.* For a moment he paused. Blood from Silas's shoe dripped upon his cheek. Silas waited, knife ready. Then, quickly, Ben pulled himself higher, watching out of the sides of his eyes.

Silas drove the knife down hard, with a grunt. Ben halfway dodged, so that the blade missed the back of his neck; but it buried to the hilt above his collarbone with a numbing shock. Leaning down, Silas jerked at the handle, trying to free the knife for another blow.

Immediately Ben seized Silas's wrist, and pulled

savagely. Silas tried to catch himself. But he had been off balance; silently he dived sidewise out of the fork, crashing through the lower branches. His fall seemed interminable. He struck the ground below with a sodden thump.

For a minute or so, the knife still deep between his shoulder bones, Ben clutched the tree with his legs and his right arm, waiting for the dizzy whirling to stop. Then he painfully inched his way down the tree to the ground, where Silas lay motionless, his head twisted grotesquely. Trouble sniffed the dead man curiously.

"Come on, dog," Ben said weakly, "we got a long way to go."

The doctor who had come down to fish the Suwannee said again to Florella, "Ma'am, I just don't know."

"How come you don't know? Ain't you a doctor?" she demanded.

He walked back to the fireplace, and looked across where Jesse Wick lay, as if asleep, his bare chest bandaged. Outside, a rooster crowed. Florella's husband threw a piece of lightwood on the fire, and lit his pipe again.

"Yes'm, I'm supposed to be a doctor, but I ain't

never seen nothing like that before, although I've heard tell of such things."

"He ain't dying?"

"How could he be, and not hardly hurt?"

"Well, why don't you do something another? He's been that way ever since Lem went and got him, after that fight day before yesterday."

"I've done treated all that ails him, except what's the matter with his brain."

"He ain't been hurt in the brain," Florella insisted.

"Ma'am, he wasn't quite right in the head, from what you say; especially lately. Hit ain't natural for no man to sit out all night and play a guitar in the cold. You ought to know that."

"He were a great one for singing and playing," she said. Then she admitted, "But that were curious, the way he done. And he always were afeered of things, though he never let on about it."

"The way it looks to me, your brother ain't bad hurt. He shore ain't dead. I'll tell you what I think. It looks to me like he just thinks he's dead," the doctor said.

"You mean he's touched?"

"Yes'm, he's touched. You've heard tell of crazy people that thinks they're God, or the

President, or something like that. Well, he just thinks he's dead, and he might as well be."

Florella and her husband stared at the doctor. Florella looked at her brother; she pulled at her fingers nervously.

"Cain't we do nothing?" she asked, finally.

"I shore don't know of nothing."

"How long you reckon he'll be like that?"

The doctor glanced at Jesse Wick, then said, "Ma'am, to tell the truth, it wouldn't surprise me none if he didn't stay just like that until the good Lord calls him shore enough."

Ben sat by the window in the sun, staring morosely at Thursday coming with the cow. The animal had broken through the rail fence last night and gone to the woods to drop the calf that now followed on weak, unsteady legs. Thursday drove them patiently, letting the cow stop often for her calf to catch up. The cow's eyes were wide, and her tight-swollen feverish bag would need hot-water cloths right away.

Hannah said, "I see he found her."

Ben said nothing, shifting his bandaged shoulder with infinite caution; every time he moved it, he could again feel the pain that had come when Thursday drew the knife out while Hannah waited with the boiling water and cobwebs.

She said, "What ails you, Ben? Is it gone to hurting again?"

"No'm. Hit's doing fine."

She moved behind him to follow Thursday with her eye, her hands gently resting on the back of Ben's chair. "Ben," she said presently, "I reckon before long it's goan be all right between me and him."

Ben's mind was in the swamp with Tom Keefer, who thought he had been betrayed; and at first he didn't realize what she had said. When his brain grasped it, he looked around quickly. "I'm shore proud to hear it, Miss Hannah."

She said, quietly, "That fellow, the one — you know — well, yesterday I heered something about him, and if it turns out to be the truth, Thursday'll have cause to know he won't never try to come back. I thought I'd tell Thursday in a day or two."

"I'm mighty glad about it."

A buggy appeared on the road, trailing a thin cloud of sandy dust. Ben watched it disinterestedly. A cold breeze stirred, and he rose and moved away from the window to sit on the couch in front of the small fire. Voices outside were audible; Thursday's and someone else's. Hannah went to the front, closing the door.

*Seem-like I ain't caused him nothing but trou-
ble; wouldn't nobody never a known where he
was at, if it hadn't been for me,* he thought miserably. *Wasn't nothing but God's own hand kept
him from gitting kilt the other day, after that
trap he thinks I led him into. I cain't blame him fer
wishing he'd a done me in to start with. But I'll
make it up to him.*

The door opened, and Julie Gordon stood
there, hesitantly, staring at him. She said, "They
told it you was stobbed in the back, and walked
all the way home with the knife still in you. I made
Amos bring me. They said you was bad off."

At first he couldn't speak, not so much from
surprise at seeing her as from astonishment at the
sudden glad pounding of his pulse. He rose
dumbly, his eyes fastened on her, feeling the
warmth that flooded him.

"Hit ain't so bad," he mumbled. "Wasn't in
my back, noway."

Julie said, "That's what she just told me."

"You might as well come on in," he said.

She stepped inside, shutting the door. Tears
slid down her wind-reddened cheeks. She smiled
at him apologetically.

"What's the matter?" Ben asked.

"You'll have to excuse me," she said.

"I shore don't see nothing to cry about," Ben said, puzzled.

"I thought you was bad off," she said. "I'm so glad you ain't, I guess I got kindly cry about it. Hit's foolish, ain't it?"

"Hit's shore that, all right. Set down, if you're a mind to."

She sat in the cowhide straight chair. "I'm sorry you and that fellow played into such hard luck. I guess now it'll come out all right, though, won't it?"

"I ain't exactly shore how it'll come out," Ben admitted. "Hit's just according to what's going on in Tom Keefer's mind. I reckon he'd take a shot at me when I go in there tomorrow, if he hadn't a lost his gun. Twicet now I've come all around balling things up. But I aim to make it up to him. We goan git him outn that swamp next time, and when he heads for Florida, I been thinking I might let my hound, Trouble, head out with him." He paused thoughtfully. "Don't know exactly how I'd go about gitting along without the old fool, but I reckon I could learn."

Her eyebrow rose, apparently of its own volition. "I know you'll hate to give him up."

255

The fire crackled. He watched her covertly, puzzling at the half-drunk feeling her nearness gave him. For a long time neither of them spoke.

Ben said, "I'm glad you come."

"Guess I had no business doing it," she said, without embarrassment.

"Hit's funny to me," he mused, "that a man ain't got much say-so about what goes on inside him. I had set my mind against such, but when you come in a while ago, I knowed my mind didn't have nothing to do with it."

She turned to face him. "What're you saying, Ben?"

"I reckon you know what I'm saying."

From the outside, Amos's voice called.

Julie rose. "I better go now, Ben."

He seized her arm with his right hand. "No, you cain't go now," he said fiercely. "Tell him you ain't coming."

She smiled at him. Then, impulsively, she kissed his mouth. He tried to pull her to him with his one arm, but she moved back.

"Ben, I got to go. What will Miss Hannah think?" she said.

"Sit down here," Ben said, "and let's try to figure out what Miss Hannah will think."

"No, Ben."

"How can you go now, after what I just told you?" he demanded angrily.

Julie studied his face. "Ben," she said, "I ain't never known quite what to make of you. That first time, at the sing, you acted kindly like you was drunk. Then you brung me them birds. After that you never come back. I ain't never bothered to hide the way it is with me. Now, coming in this way on you, hit'd be kind of natural for you to make up to a girl."

"You've got everything thought out too good."

"It ain't that, Ben. Don't look so mad."

Miss Hannah opened the door and said, "Your brother said tell you he was going down to the barn to help Thursday doctor that cow, and he'd be back in a little bit." She closed the door again.

Ben said, bitterly, "Now I guess you aim to drive on off and leave him, you're in such a powerful hurry to git away from me."

For a moment she stood there. Then she sank down beside him. He sat sullenly, staring at the fire. She kissed him on the neck, gently.

Still he made no move, and she kissed his ear. A fire began creeping through his veins. He looked at her; a tiny smile moved her lips. Ben drew her tight against him with his good arm, and he kissed her savagely. He breathed the hot breath that came from her lungs, and it was sweet and heady.

Presently she pushed back.

"Don't move!" he said fiercely, holding her against him.

"My God, Ben," she whispered, "I got to!"

"You'll go out."

"No, I won't. I'll sit right yonder."

"Don't go! Stay right here next to me."

"I *cain't*, Ben. *Please*, Ben, let me loose. I won't go," she whispered. "Let me sit over there a minute."

"All right, if that's the way you want to act," he said angrily.

She stood in front of the fire for a moment, with her back toward him. He said nothing. Then she sat in a chair and straightened her skirt.

"I look a sight," she said. Her eyebrow lifted.

Ben felt a grin on his face. "There goes that eyebrow again," he said. They sat in silence. Then Ben said, "You know, I'm gitting plumb satisfied to have you over there, long's I can look at you. That's curious, ain't it? I'd like to just squeeze you so tight you'd holler, but I don't have it to do. I can sit right here, and there's a fire in my blood right on, only it's lower burning, hot as ever but without so much smoke," he mused. "If you had gone on out while ago when you started to, I do believe it would a killed me. What makes love do that to a sensible man, you reckon?"

"I don't want to never go out and leave you, Ben."

"When I come back outn the swamp this next time, I aim to fix it where you cain't," he said. He rose and kissed her hair, and said, apologetically, "I didn't mean to talk to you the way I done while ago."

Going into the swamp again, with Thursday paddling him and Trouble asleep in the bow, Ben remembered that first time he penetrated it. The place had been green then, and it was summer, and the gators were everywhere. Thursday kept watching the great flocks of waterfowl that now crisscrossed the white sky, tier upon tier of them, and staring at the colonnades of mighty cypresses. *Maybe he'll trap some with me later on*, Ben thought.

"I'm shore much oblige you offered to paddle

me in," Ben said again. "Don't reckon I could a made it by myself for quite a spell."

The first time he had come into Okefenokee it had been to find his lost hound; now he was going to give him away. He wondered uneasily where Tom Keefer would be, and what he would do. *I'll find out them answers before long now.*

They landed on the lower end of the island, about a half mile from the old campsite. Trouble bounded ashore and began sniffing about, his tail busy.

"You don't want me to go along with you?" Thursday asked.

"If he seen two of us coming, he'd hit for the back end of the swamp," Ben said. "Me and this old hound will be back after while, and Tom Keefer along with us on his way to Florida."

As Ben walked along, Trouble ran ahead. Once he stopped, trailing busily, and then eight wild turkeys got up with a great booming of wings, to fly swiftly across the palmetto-and-pine flatland and sail down in a distant thicket, almost out of sight. Later a bunch of ringnecks flushed off a little cypress pond, and from nowhere a duck hawk plummeted down with blinding swiftness, to level off over the ducks and competently sink his steel into a speeding drake.

260

At the camp, Keefer was not in sight. But he had been there; the black butts of firewood lay beyond the last fire Ben had built.

It was the hound who found Keefer, lying near the bank, where he had pulled himself trying to reach water. Now he lay, half-propped against the butt of a tree, his red-shot eyes open. Fever had wrung his body dry of moisture, and his lips were burned dry.

Keefer's eyes focused slowly, and he mumbled, "Git me some water, Ben."

Dumbly Ben went to the water's edge. Keefer drank, then Ben laid a wet cloth over the dry forehead. Keefer's face was yellowed beneath his thin beard, except for an unhealthy redness at his cheeks. But what Ben tried not to see was the bloated bulge of his middle, where Silas Dorson's second bullet had torn through the swamp man's side and out his lower belly.

Ben's chin trembled. "I never thought to find you in no fix like this."

He kept giving him water, and presently Keefer said, painfully, "I'm glad you come. I didn't want to peep down the well and leave you thinking I blamed you fer it." His words came with an agonized slowness. For the moment at least his brain was clear.

"I never had nothing to do with it, if that's what you mean," Ben muttered. "But I guess I was to blame, one way or another."

A joree ran upon the ground near by, chirping curiously. Keefer said, "When it first happened, I figured it was your doings, but after I come back I knowed it wasn't so. . . . You was trying to help me out, Ben. Hit just come about that way. If you had wanted to git shed of me . . . you wouldn't had to be so round-about. When a man's trapped-like . . . he don't . . . have time to study nothing out . . ."

He breathed heavily. Trouble had gone to sleep, stretched out.

After a while, Keefer said, "I kindly wisht you'd go on back."

"I cain't leave you here to die right by your-self."

Keefer licked his lips with a dry tongue. "Hit's the way I'd ruther have it. You can come back and lay me under." He struggled with the words, pausing as if he had forgotten what he was talk-ing about. "Ain't no use to look so tore-up about it. At first it were a . . . disappointmint the way it turnt out. Then I kept gitting . . . worse off . . . and I knowed I was on my last go-round

2 6 2

. . . and I begin to wonder what dying was like. I done many a different thing . . . but this here's . . . a new one on me . . . and I've got so curious I cain't hardly wait."

The joree flew up into the brown tendrils of a bullace vine. Keefer said, "I've laid here studying on it . . . one day after another . . . wondering where-at you go to, and what *hit's* like. Some says one thing and some . . . says another. But you got to see fer yourself to know. Maybe there ain't nothing at all to it . . . just dead. Er maybe it's the way they say . . . them as has put they minds on it. Er maybe it's such a to-do as no man . . . ever dreamt of."

Ben said, heavily, "I had counted on letting my old hound go to Florida with you, after I balled things up that way."

"Don't expect it's . . . Florida . . . I'm a-going to this time."

Keefer's eyes were half-closed, speculative. Ben turned away, hesitantly. He walked a little way and looked back. Trouble still slept. Ben started to call him, then thought, *I could git him when I come back tomorrow. Just let him stay with him until then.* He walked on. After a while he began running.

THE END

Breinigsville, PA USA
01 September 2010
244747BV00001B/64/P